CRAVE

EVERNIGHT PUBLISHING ®

www.evernightpublishing.com

SAM CRESCENT

Copyright© 2022

Sam Crescent

Editor: Karyn White

Cover Art: Sour Cherry Designs

Jacket Design: Jay Aheer

ISBN: 978-1-77339-710-8

CRAVE

CRAVE

Trojans MC, 8

Sam Crescent

Copyright © 2017

Chapter One

It had been another long day at Vale Valley hospital, and Kasey Lintel just wanted to get to her apartment, have a long bath, and go to sleep. She didn't even care for food right at that moment. Another long day, and this time, the Grim Reaper himself had won way too many times. She'd counted six deaths today. Seeing their families cry and sob had been too much for her, reminding her of the pain of losing her last surviving family member, her brother. *That* pain had been unlike anything she'd ever felt before in her life.

She watched the floor numbers change as the elevator took her home.

Her neck hurt from being in the same position for most of the day. Her feet were killing her, and if that wasn't enough, she felt like she'd done nothing but try to stop crying.

When the elevator came to a stop, she breathed a sigh of relief, climbing off to make her way toward her apartment door. Before she could get inside, Lindsey, her busty blonde neighbor, came out of her apartment, carrying a large bouquet of roses.

"They look nice," Kasey said.

Lindsey always had way too much energy, which was probably why she spent a lot of time with different men. The walls were rather thin, so Kasey got to hear all the dirty activity going on. Sometimes she was envious of the easy sex that her neighbor got. Kasey couldn't have that. Most of the guys she'd dated always told her she was the kind of girl they'd take to see their parents. Rarely did she get to the bedroom department before she'd been pulled into something fun, and that just sucked.

So in the last ten years, she'd had five boyfriends with only one of them ending up in sex. At thirty years old, she'd been with one guy, lost her virginity to him, and it was only when he didn't want her to go to medical school that they broke up. Boy, had they been at cross purposes.

He'd wanted her barefoot and pregnant.

She'd wanted a career and to help people. Fortunately, her brother had been there. He'd told her to not let a guy hold her back from what she wanted. She missed him.

"They are so nice," Lindsey said. "And they're for you."

"Me?"

"Yep, that's right. The delivery man was so sweet. He was totally like, these flowers are not for you, miss, but they're for your lady neighbor. He thought I'd have a fit because they weren't for me."

"Right," Kasey said, staring at the flowers. "This is the second lot, right?"

"Yep. First lot came yesterday, but I've been so

nosy, and I'm so sorry. I couldn't wait for you to find out who it is. You have the strangest friends. Yesterday you got them from Pie. Today they're from Chip. Is it a little joke?"

"I don't know. It's their names. Something to do with a road name I believe." She recalled Crazy telling her about it while he'd been watching Leanna after his vicious ex shot her.

Kasey tended to stay away from bikers, and the Trojans MC were the real deal. Bike riding, dangerous men, and she had no interest in that.

The parents of Holly, one of the MC women, had gotten killed because of some past association with the mafia. At least that's what Kasey heard at the funeral when she went to pay her respects.

"OMG! You're telling me you've got some bikers wanting you."

The excitement was bubbling up inside Lindsey.

Opening her apartment door, Kasey invited Lindsey inside. She was kind of a friend. They had nothing in common, but she found when misery seemed to take up residence, Lindsey didn't allow it to happen.

"I've never been to a biker party. I want to meet them. They all look badass and dangerous with those leather jackets and tattoos."

Kasey pointed toward the kitchen counter as she filled her kettle with water. Lindsey took a seat but spent most of it bouncing on one spot. Her tits pressed against the front of her shirt, showing that she didn't wear a bra.

Kasey didn't know why she noticed her friend's lack of bra, but she did.

"I've never been to a party either. There's a club in Vale Valley. I work at the hospital there."

"You totally have to introduce me."

"I don't think that will happen."

Lindsey got out of her seat and took the card, leaning in close as Kasey removed her jacket.

"Look, look, this guy Chip wants you to make a date. There's his cell phone number. 'Pretty flowers for a beautiful woman. Thank you for all that you do. I was hoping you'd like to do dinner sometime.'"

Lindsey read out the card, and Kasey recalled the card the other day. Something along the lines of, "Totally dig you. We can have some fun times. Call me."

She'd thought they were all a joke, and now it seemed like it totally wasn't.

"You've got to call them, and then you can take me to handle one of the men, or I get to watch you totally be taken by two men."

Once again, her neighbor giggled, and Kasey rolled her eyes, not really sure on what to do.

"I'm sure they've got the wrong person."

The kettle began to wheeze, letting her knew it was time for tea.

She poured Lindsey a cup, then herself, afterward taking a seat at her table.

"I'm so green with envy right now."

"Don't be."

"I've been living next door to you for a couple of years now, Kasey, and I've noticed you rarely have anyone come to take you out on a date. These two men want to get freaky with you." Lindsey shook her breasts as she said that. "Go for it. What have you got to lose?"

"I'm not like that. I've never been like that."

"Maybe you need to start living a little. I don't imagine for a second it's all fun and games at the hospital. Your eyes are puffy from crying. Bad day?"

It was a bit much for her when her neighbor was the only one who noticed.

"Tough."

"We only live once, and if you take life way too seriously, you're going to spend the rest of your life regretting it. I speak from experience here."

"You're twenty-one."

"Actually, I'm twenty-six years old, and I've had so much fun living it up. I have no plans to be tied down until I'm ready. There's just so much to experience, ya know? Why do guys only get to pick and choose about all the fish in the sea? I want it just as much, and I'm going to taste every single guy I want."

"Aren't you worried about earning a reputation?"

"Meh, I don't care. This is what I hate. Men screw a bunch of women and are called studs."

"We call them man-whores."

"A woman sleeps with guys and she's a whore or a slut. Double standards. I love cock. I'm not too picky about my pussy either if you ever want to go."

Kasey burst out laughing. "You're a hoot."

"I've got some serious tongue action going. Believe me. I could make you scream, if you're worried about being called a slut, which by the way, anyone does call you that, tell them to come to me. I'll put them straight."

Kasey couldn't stop laughing. "Thank you. I really needed to laugh tonight."

"That's what I'm here for. I should totally charge you, but you make the best tea ever." Lindsey finished her drink. "I'm afraid I've got to cut the party short tonight. I've got a date, and I'm going to live it up. Wish me luck that this guy not only has a big dick but also knows how to use it."

"I will keep my fingers crossed for you."

"There's nothing more disappointing than a hard cock with a really bad driver. You know what I mean? Just because it's hard and big doesn't mean you stick it in, and there you go, good sex."

She didn't say anything else, following Lindsey to the door to say goodnight.

Closing and locking her door afterward, Kasey leaned against it, pulling out her cell phone to dial Crazy's number. She had his number after he kept coming to the hospital for advice with regards to illnesses and sickness.

Instead of him constantly making the trek, she'd told him to call her.

"Hello, Kasey, makes a change for you to be phoning me."

She chuckled. "Yeah, I guess. I'm kind of confused. I've received two bouquets of flowers. One from Chip, and another from Pie." She bit her lip. "Is this because of something? I don't know."

"They're trying to woo you."

"Woo me?"

"Yes. They're asking for a date I take it."

"I think so."

"They saw you and they liked you, Kasey."

"Oh."

"Don't sound so shocked. You're a beautiful woman."

"Thank you. I think." Crazy was completely devoted to his woman, Leanna. Even though he'd paid her a compliment, there was nothing else in it.

"Would you like me to put a stop to their shit? Is it bothering you?"

"No, it's fine. I just wanted to make sure they didn't feel obliged or anything."

"Nope, nothing like that."

She asked him how Leanna and the kids were doing before hanging up. Staring at the two bouquets of flowers, she couldn't help but smile. They really were beautiful.

****

Chip sat staring at his beer bottle, wondering if going to visit Kasey was out of the question. It had taken him three hours to pick the right flowers that he thought would really stand out and show their beauty.

Pretty flowers paled in comparison to the beautiful woman. From the moment he first saw her a few years ago at the hospital, to only a month ago at the funeral, she'd captivated him. What pissed him off now was Pie's interest.

Chip had held off going to see her for some time as he didn't know what her thoughts were about bikers or the MC life.

Trojans MC didn't have the best reputation, especially after the recent showdown with the mafia. Everyone was in a fucking state. Russ and Sheila had been killed, and because of it, Duke had gone after Anton Abelli.

There had been tension ever since.

Since the deaths of her parents, Holly had withdrawn herself from club life, staying at home with the kids. Duke didn't look much better either, and from what he'd heard, the blog that Mary and Holly set up wasn't faring well either.

They'd not made a post in nearly two months, and their followers were starting to worry.

Pushing all those worries to one side, Chip focused on his beer, which he'd not taken a sip from.

The main door of the clubhouse swung open, and he saw Crazy step into the room. Crazy clocked Pie, who had a club whore all over him, and then turned to Chip.

"What the fuck is going on with you two?" Crazy asked.

Chip looked at Pie then back at Crazy. "What?"

"I've just had a call from Kasey. Guess what, she's had two bouquets of flowers, and wondered what the hell they were."

Rage filled Chip as he got out of his seat, advancing toward Pie, who in turn pushed the bitch off his lap and stood.

"What the fuck are you doing?" Chip asked.

"I was sending flowers to a woman that deserves them," Pie said, standing toe to toe.

"Deserves them? You were close to having another woman's mouth wrapped around your limp dick."

"No, I wouldn't."

Chip sneered at Pie. "Stay away from Kasey. She's mine."

"She's not anyone's. I actually consider her a friend, and she's been through a hell of a lot. I would really prefer it if none of you fucked up what friendship I have with her." Crazy pointed at the both of them.

Turning to Crazy, Chip glared. "If I want to see her, I'll fucking see her, and no one is ever going to tell me differently." He stepped away from Pie and shook his head.

Crazy grabbed him.

"I'm not going to hurt her."

Seconds passed, and finally Crazy let him go.

"You really think you're going to win her?" Pie asked. "I sent a bouquet of flowers yesterday."

"She won't want your skanky ass, especially as all you seem to be doing is dropping your dick into anything that will have you."

"This is not something you both should be doing," Crazy said. "She helps the club, and I call her whenever I need help with Strawberry and Luke."

"Stop being a pussy," Pie said. "Chip and I will

handle this. You've got nothing to worry about."

Chip wasn't interested in listening to Pie. Leaving the clubhouse, he went toward his bike, straddling the machine.

Crazy had followed him outside, and he looked toward the brother. He was a crazy son of a bitch, and Chip had no interest in getting on his bad side. The club was at a tipping point from the Abelli interference. Right now, they had to be stronger than ever before.

"I'm not going to hurt her. I've no interest in fucking with her, like Pie is in there. I like her." What he wouldn't admit to Crazy was the fact he'd been watching her for some time.

Even before the funeral. At the hospital he'd noticed her, but he'd not been ready to accept his feelings. He'd finally realized that he wanted her, and there was no way he'd let Crazy or Pie take that away from him.

Turning over his ignition, he didn't give Crazy a chance to say or do anything else as he pulled out of the clubhouse parking lot. His anger slowly ebbed away with every second he put between himself and the club, especially Pie.

Knowing that fucker had actually sent her a bouquet only pissed him off more. Pie had no right to her.

Speeding up, Chip found himself riding toward her apartment, and after thirty minutes on the road, he parked his bike, staring up the length of the building. He knew her apartment number, and deciding to take matters into his own hands, he climbed off his bike and made his way into the building.

Instead of taking the elevator, he took the stairs. He'd never been nervous talking to a woman before. He wasn't any saint, and never claimed to be perfect; far from it. Being in the Trojans MC he'd done a lot of crazy shit. Fucked many women he couldn't even remember the name of, but always bagging his dick up before he stuck it anywhere. Women didn't mean anything to him. Only the patch he wore, and his loyalty to the club. He made sure the old ladies had his respect, but that was as far as he went. Kasey wasn't a club whore, nor a woman who seemed to be looking for a biker.

She was all woman. A nurse. A woman who cared.

He'd seen the love in her eyes as she took care of patients, witnessed it with Leanna, and then at the funeral. Kasey cared.

Standing in front of her door, he didn't hold back, knocking on the hard wood, waiting for her to answer.

It was quite late, but he needed an answer to his question.

Seconds later, Kasey opened the door. Her long brown hair was tied up in a bun, and she wore a fluffy blue robe with the belt wrapped around her waist.

"Hi," she said.

"I don't know if you remember me. The name's Chip." He stuck his hand out, and she didn't hesitate to take it, giving it a shake.

Her smile had his gut twisting, and damn it if he didn't want to kiss those plump lips. They'd look good wrapped around his dick. The very thought had his cock thickening, and he quickly put the image to bed. He didn't need to be thinking about those lips anywhere on his body.

"I remember." She pointed behind her. "The flowers are really beautiful. Thank you."

"You're welcome." He rubbed the back of his head. "Do you want to go out?"

She frowned. "Now?"

"No, not right now. Do you want to go out on a date with me?"

A loud, feminine scream filled the air. Kasey bit her lip, and her cheeks went bright red.

"Do you have company?" he asked.

"That is *not* me. I'm alone. That's my neighbor." She stepped back. "Would you like to come in?"

"Yes, I would."

He stepped over the threshold as moaning once again filled the air. Kasey chuckled. "You know, I thought she'd come home alone. I guess I was wrong."

"You hear your neighbor often?"

"She likes to entertain. Not that she's a prostitute or anything. I like Lindsey. She's really nice."

Following her into the kitchen, he saw the bouquet of roses he'd picked out, along with the ones Pie sent.

His looked way better, but then he'd spent ages picking the perfect flowers.

"Would you like a drink?"

"Love one," he said, wishing she didn't wear such a large robe so that he could look at her generous curves.

"How's Holly and everyone doing?" she asked.

He sighed. "Not so good. I've not seen Holly since the funeral. She's really not interested in club life at all."

Even though it was selfish of him, he didn't want to talk about Holly.

"It can be hard losing a loved one and a family member."

He knew it was only Kasey now. Her brother dying some time ago had left her the only surviving Lintel.

"I'm sorry for your loss."

She smiled, but he saw the sadness once again in her eyes. "It happens." She sighed. "So, a date?"

This time he did smile. "I hope you don't think it's rude me asking."

"It's not rude to ask, is it?"

He saw the laughter. "No, last time I checked asking for a date rather than taking one is very grownup and manly. It's what I'm all about."

She chuckled. "Then after you've gone through all this trouble. I'll have to say yes."

He felt on top of the fucking world.

Chapter Two

The following day Kasey stood looking at the board where the doctor had ticked off his latest rounds. She had to follow up every hour to keep an eye on the patients' monitors. Making her way to each room, she smiled at the patient, spoke with them, had a bit of a laugh with those that she recalled seeing often, and marked off their chart. Most of the time she loved her job. She loved helping bring families together, and to watch that joy spread as they realized the person would live.

Then of course, the days when they lost patients were the worst. She hated it more than anything else in the world. Being professional sucked those days.

She always felt their pain, but she'd been told not to cry with them, just to tell them the news and leave them to their grief.

Kasey had stood in a room after being told her brother didn't make it. No one wrapped their arms around her. She'd stood alone, lost, and frightened.

Pushing those thoughts aside, she finished her rounds, and was about to leave for her lunch when she heard her name being called.

"Kasey, yo, Kasey."

She turned to see Pie making his way toward her.

"Hello," she said, stopping. She glanced behind him. "Do you have a friend or someone needing to be seen?"

"No, nothing like that. I came to see you." He stopped right in front of her. A huge smile filled his face, and she couldn't help but respond. Even though sadness played heavily in her work, she tried to fight it every single day with happy thoughts. Some days were better than others, but Pie seemed to have an ease about him that just made her think of fun.

"Two Trojan boys in two days," she said.

"Chip saw you?"

"Yes, last night." She locked her fingers together, and waited. "What can I do for you?"

"Did you get my flowers?"

"I did. They're very beautiful. Thank you so much for taking the time." Her stomach chose that moment to growl, and she winced.

"Long day, huh?"

"Something like that."

"Come on. I'll take you to lunch. My treat."

She was surprised when they left the hospital and she saw him move toward a large, gleaming motorcycle. She shook her head. "No, no, no, I can't get on that."

"Why not? I drive safely."

"That's a death trap. Can we take my car?"

"You don't want to enjoy the ride of your life?" he asked with a wink.

"Not really. Maybe another day. Can we take my car?"

He rolled his eyes. "You know I'm determined now to get you on the back of my bike."

"My brother used to ride a bike." She didn't know why she blurted it out, but for some reason, it seemed important. His bike was the only one she'd ridden on, and she loved every second of it. He always told her though that no matter what anyone said, she was only ever to ride on the back of someone she trusted.

It took skill to ride a bike.

She wasn't about to impart his advice to Pie. The last thing she wanted was to make him upset.

"I won't push about that. Come on, I wanted you to have a good lunch, not be feeling sad or anything.

Shit, I'm sorry. That sounded cold, didn't it? I'm not good with all this stuff. I'm used to people dying around me, and there I go putting my foot in my mouth."

"It's fine. Honestly, it's fine."

She found his concern and rambling rather endearing. He looked … worried, which was strange. Pie always seemed the most collected of all the bikers.

He took her keys, and they walked toward her car.

Pie opened the door for her, and she thanked him, getting inside.

Seeing the large man inside her rather small car made her chuckle even harder.

"You're finding this really funny?"

"It just doesn't look right seeing you there. I'm sorry." She covered her mouth, but when he had to adjust the seat, she couldn't help it, and the laughter overcame her.

He joined her, and for several moments they sat in her car laughing until tears were running down her face. She wiped them away, shaking her head. "I've not laughed like that in a long time."

"Then I'm glad I amuse you."

Pie finally got comfortable, and they headed in to Vale Valley. She lived not too far from the hospital, but not inside the actual biker town. She'd visited it a few times as it was in fact a nice area to live in.

She remembered reading somewhere that the overall crime rate was actually rather low, and she put that down to the MC living there.

He took her to a place called Mac's Diner.

"This used to have Mary's name on it, but after some serious shit went down that nearly cost her Pike, she pulled away from Mac and the diner," Pie said.

"Right, okay."

Pie led the way, and they took two seats near the window. She reached for the menu, and Pie shook his head. "Try the burgers. It's why I come here. They're so good. They're second place to Holly and Mary's, but I've not eaten anything they've cooked in a few weeks now, and I'm in serious withdrawal."

Thinking about Holly, Kasey put the menu down. "She's still not coming around after everything that happened?"

"The death of her parents is really hitting her hard. I can't tell you everything, but you were at the funeral." Pie shrugged. "None of us know what to do."

"It's hard. Losing not one but all of your parents. You can go to a dark place, and that can be a hole that you can never get out of."

"Did you go to a dark place?"

"Yes. It frightened me." She bit her lip, wondering if she should tell him the full extent of the damage. "I, erm, I was studying to be a nurse when I lost my brother. The doctors, nothing could save him, and I remember feeling helpless. I wanted to be a nurse to help people. To be a little light in a really shitty day, and when no one could save him, I figured it was crap. I still studied, and I went through the motions. I worked, and I got through my classes. The fire I once had was gone. You know. Totally extinguished. Anyway, my depression hit me, and I no longer wanted to feel the pain, and being the person I was, I tried to score a hit."

Pie's eyes went wide. "You went looking for drugs."

"I went looking for drugs. I'd seen what they did. The total oblivion. I was jealous, and I wanted that kind of hit. I wanted to forget. I had everything prepared. I remember heating it up so that it was liquid, my arm was prepared. I'd found a vein and gotten the needle. I was just about to stick it into my arm, and I just stopped. In a strange way, it was like I could see myself through my brother's eyes. He was dead, long dead, but I stared at what I was about to do, and I was horrified. I threw the needle away, and I curled up in a ball, crying, completely at my lowest point, but knowing I couldn't let myself get worse."

"Your brother's memory saved you."

"Yeah, it really did."

"Wow, totally hard-ass. I have to say you wouldn't be sitting in front of me now if you were a user. The club doesn't take drugs. They're not allowed, and if anyone does them, Duke's all over their ass. Their patch is taken."

"Drugs ruin lives a hell of a lot more than people realize. I've seen some of the patients, and it's not pretty." Their burgers arrived, and the smell was so amazing.

"Thanks," Pie said, picking up his burger. "Now, there's an art to eating this burger right."

"Okay."

"You hold it like this." He held the burger with two hands. She did. "Then you open your mouth."

She laughed. "You're kidding, right?"

"No. Open. Come on. You're in company of a man who is dying here for another burger. Come on."

She rolled her eyes, opened her mouth, and watched as Pie shoved it into his mouth. "Do it," he said, his mouth stuffed.

Shaking her head, she opened her mouth once again and stuffed the burger inside, taking a large bite. There was more in there than she could chew.

"Good, right?" he asked. His mouth full, but he was able to push it down one cheek as he spoke.

"Very good," she said, copying him.

****

Chip was ready in his suit, and as he made his way toward her building for their date, he wanted this to be perfect. Pie had already come home and told him about the amazing burger they had at Mac's Diner, and even though he was pissed, he discovered that she'd not agreed to a date. They'd just had lunch together.

"Well, hello, handsome," a busty blonde said.

He smiled at her and took the elevator, which she slid into.

"Are you coming to see me?" she asked.

"No, I'm not."

"Now that's a pity. I know most people on this floor, and I've never seen you before so I'm guessing you're the date for the night?"

She stood a little too close for his liking.

"With all due respect, could you back up?"

She held her hands up. "Sorry, I know everyone on my floor, and seeing as you clicked the same floor as me, I was curious."

Wanting her to shut up, he looked toward her. "I'm going to see Kasey."

"Kasey. Oh my, are you like one of those MC guys that have been sending her flowers?" She was clapping her hands, and any interest seemed to change direction.

"The name's Chip," he said.

"That's it. You're the one with the most beautiful bouquet. Kasey's eyes lit right up when she saw them. I'm Lindsey by the way. Her very good neighbor."

"You're the noisy neighbor."

"Oh, dear, you heard that? I do try to be quiet, and I've told Kasey many times to come and give me a knock, and I'll tone it down. I tell you, some guys just know what to do with it, and this guy was huge, and he knew. I felt I'd hit the jackpot, and then the guy came in like five minutes. Jackpot sucked big time. He couldn't even get it straight up again. I was so lonely. Speaking of lonely, do you have a lot of really hot, really well-hung guys at the club?"

He frowned. "I don't spend a lot of times checking guys' dicks out."

"That's a real shame. If you have a party can I be Kasey's plus one?" Lindsey asked.

Chip had never known a woman like her. He'd known of women talking all day long but not the kind that told him everything about their personal lives. They had pussy back at the club, but he hadn't used that in some time.

He'd not been interested in tapping any of them.

"Kasey will be *my* plus one."

"Is it serious already? I should have known. If you ever need an extra in the bedroom count me in. Her body is fucking smokin'. I love those tits of hers as well. They look like the kind that would be heaven with a cock pressed between them."

"You're bisexual?" he asked. He was very much aware of how hot and sexy Kasey's curvy body was. She wasn't thin—he'd put her between a size sixteen and eighteen. He loved her large tits, thick thighs, and rounded stomach. Her ass was also a big deal for him. He loved watching her bend over, and it took every single ounce of strength inside him not to caress that beauty.

"Honey, I'm a woman who just wants to enjoy life and never say never." She winked at him.

The elevator doors opened, and they were heading toward Kasey's door.

"Tell Kasey she's a lucky woman."

Lindsey was gone by the time he knocked on Kasey's door. When he saw her in a black cocktail dress, he was blown away. The dress hugged her curves, showcasing her amazing tits and hips.

He was tempted to cancel dinner and go straight to the dessert, but he didn't want to be rude.

"Am I overdressed?" she asked, running her hands down her thighs.

"No. You look beautiful."

"You texted to dress for somewhere fancy, and I don't exactly have a wardrobe for all of that." Her brown hair was in curls and cascaded down around her.

Chip was taken aback by how long her hair actually was, down past her breasts to her stomach.

She usually kept it either in a bun or a ponytail at the back of her head, which he realized she looped it so the length always seemed shorter.

"How do I look?" he asked, giving her a twirl. He loved her little giggle.

"I have to say rather dashing in a tux." She stepped forward, her hand brushing over his shoulder. "Just some fluff."

"Are you ready to go?"

"Yes, I am." She grabbed her purse, and he waited while she locked the door.

Taking her hand, he made his way toward the elevator once again. "I met your neighbor?"

"Lindsey?"

"Yes. She says to tell you that you're a lucky woman."

"Did she ask for an invite to one of your parties?"

He laughed. "She told me she'd be your plus one."

"That's Lindsey. I know she's a bit … different, but I like her. Even though she's wacky in the coolest sense ever, I think she's got a really kind heart."

"She was telling about her date and how he didn't

go for long enough and couldn't get it up."

Kasey groaned. "That was her date the other night. She was worried because she didn't want him to disappoint."

"Let's not talk about her date right now." His cock was already thickening, and not for Lindsey either. No, thinking about sex with Kasey close and her floral scent were driving him crazy.

He wanted her.

Taking her outside to his waiting car, she paused. "This is yours?"

"Yes. It belongs to the club really. We can all drive it."

"I thought you came here on your bike."

"Not with this tux on. This is my special dating one." He winked at her. "I can drive, and I heard Pie saying that you're not comfortable driving on the back of a bike."

"Oh, thank you."

"I'm not going to force you to do something you really don't want to do." He opened the door. "For my lady."

She took his hand, and slid into the passenger side.

Rounding to the driver's side, he willed himself to get under control. He felt like a damn teenager on his first date.

He'd never taken a woman on a date. Being part of the Trojans for most of his life, the pussy had been free, and he didn't have any reason to take that on a date when it was always freely offered.

Climbing behind the wheel, he started the engine.

"Pie came while I was on a lunch break. I hope that's okay. He took us to Mac's Diner thingy, and he was really craving some good burgers."

"Mary's not been around as much since Holly's become a recluse," he said. "Mac's like second best."

He drove away from Vale Valley, heading toward the city where he'd booked them into an Italian restaurant.

"How was work?"

"It was fine. I'm actually thinking of taking some vacation time. I've got a few days off next week, and I was going to see how I felt."

"Has it been rough?"

"Rough as can be. I don't know if I should change positions, find something smaller, locally, you know? It's a thought, but then I don't want to get bored, and being in the hospital means I'm always busy."

"Crazy praises you often. He believes you're really amazing, and I don't think he knows what he'd do without you. You should charge him every time he calls you up."

"It's no trouble at all. I don't mind the conversation or helping him when one of his babies is sick, or even when Leanna is sick. Most of the time it's home remedies like honey and lemon, or just nipping to the pharmacy to grab a few over the counter items."

"You're too nice."

She laughed. "I'm a nurse, I'm supposed to be nice."

Pulling up outside of the restaurant, he shook his head at the valet who had been about to open the door on his woman. He had no intention of sharing, not tonight. It was bad enough Pie wanted a piece of her.

There were a lot of things he wanted to share with the club, but his woman wasn't one of them.

Taking Kasey's hand, he led her inside, and the maître d' escorted them to the table he'd reserved. It was one Duke always reserved when he took Holly on a date.

It offered them privacy, and Chip wanted that.

"This is a really nice place," she said.

"Did you think I had some shack in mind?"

"I didn't know you liked Italian, and I'm a simple kind of girl. Shack, restaurant, dive, so long as the food is good, I really don't care."

Her smile sparked, and it made Chip want to kiss her. The feelings she evoked inside him were so strong.

His cock was already hardening, but it was more than just sex. He loved being around her.

The waiter came with the menus, and he glanced through it, ordering some wine for Kasey and water for himself.

"It's okay. I'll just have the water."

"I don't mind you drinking."

"And I always found drinking to be a little boring by myself."

"You don't drink at home?" he asked.

"Nope. You're driving tonight, and I'm not going to touch a drop."

"You'll have to invite me to dinner so that we can enjoy a drink."

"I may just do that."

Chapter Three

Kasey laughed at Chip's retelling of Pike's reaction to Mary going into labor, how panicked he was. He made funny faces, weird noises, and she couldn't help but laugh as she enjoyed her bowl of chicken soup.

"You guys always strike me as being a family. Like nothing can get between you."

Sadness washed over his face, and she regretted her words instantly. "Normally, we are. At the moment we're heading toward a crisis point. I can't go into the details. It's a club thing."

"And I'm not part of the club."

"Unless you want to skip the entire process and go straight into being my old lady?"

She smiled. "I'd love to say yes, but, erm, can we do the dating thing first?" She didn't want to upset him. Chip was really nice. She really enjoyed his company, but she wouldn't jump straight into a relationship just because of it.

"I'm only *partly* kidding. I'm a good catch. You should listen to your neighbor."

"I'll take that under advisement. She's been in love ten times this year alone."

"I'm the exception to the rule," he said. "I'm a hot catch."

"Of that I have no doubt at all. You're a very good catch, which makes me wonder why I'm sitting opposite you." She leaned forward a little, and so did he.

"I don't know why we're whispering, but I think you just put yourself down."

"I'm kind of boring. I work all kinds of hours at the hospital. I'm not considered a catch."

"I think you're very beautiful. You clean up

nicely, and I enjoy being around you." He reached out, stroking her cheek. "Don't put yourself down so much."

"So what exactly do you do at the club?"

"What job?"

"Yeah."

"I work wherever I'm needed. Most of the time I take care of business at the mechanic shop." He waved his hands. "I'm good at fixing things. If your car ever needs to have a look over it, give me a call or drop by. We're always willing to help a woman out."

"I'll remember that."

"I'm not a businessman, and I don't have some special mad skill. I'm a simple man at heart. I love good food. The men at the club are like brothers to me. I'm loyal to them and my patch."

"You'd die for them?"

"Yes."

She tucked some hair behind her ear. "I miss that about having a family."

"What?"

"Having someone you know you could trust, love, die for."

"Were you close with your family?" he asked.

"Yes, I was. So very close. My parents died in a car accident when I was fifteen. I was terrified that I'd end up in a home or something. My brother was there though." She smiled. "We were sitting at the hospital. Child services were waiting to take me away, and he said to me, 'Kasey, you promise me not to give me any shit. You go to school, no drugs or wild parties. Promise me.' I promised him, and I was able to stay with him."

"Sounds like a pretty decent brother to me."

"He was the best. When he died, it made it even more terrible." She smiled.

Chip reached across the table, taking her hand.

"You're not alone. You may think you're alone, but you're not. I can promise you that. You've got me, Crazy, Leanna, Strawberry, Luke, the club."

She thought it was really sweet of him, but she knew that in the scheme of things, she didn't really have the club.

"Let's not make this date morbid. You know the nitty-gritty details of my life, so let's move on." The soup no longer appealed to her.

Next, pasta.

She loved pasta, and from Chip's reaction he did as well. "So, I heard that each guy has their own road name or something like that. Crazy once told me it's because when he's pushed too far, there's no stopping him. He's crazy."

"He told you that?"

She nodded. "Yep, one day when I visited, and Leanna mentioned it."

"I had a chip on my shoulder when I was younger. One of the guys, ha, Russ as it happens, gave me the nickname 'Chip.' I had a chip on my shoulder. It would always be, 'Chip, grab me a beer.' 'Chip, go empty the trash.' Chip. He gave me the name. Pie is obvious. He loves pies. I mean the brother is obsessed with them. Whenever Mary and Holly are experimenting with pies, they'll call him. He's like their expert."

"What's your real name?" she asked.

"My real name?"

"Yep, I'd like to know it."

"You'll prefer Chip."

She laughed. "Just tell me."

"Rufus Jones."

Silence fell between them, and for some reason, she just couldn't help but laugh, covering her mouth as she did. "Rufus Jones?"

"Yes, I told you you'd prefer Chip."

"It just doesn't seem right, you know. I was expecting a David or a Larry."

"It's Rufus."

She held her hand out. "Well hello, Rufus. I'm Kasey." He shook her hand.

"You're enjoying this."

"No, it's nice to know who I'm with."

"It's not a mystery. You can ask me whatever you want, and I'll answer it."

She twirled her fork in the spaghetti and thought of some questions. "What do you like to do in your spare time?"

"Take beautiful women out for Italian food, ride my bike, party, have some fun. Take in the sights."

"You like sightseeing?"

"Occasionally. I can certainly be talked into it. What about you?"

"I love sightseeing. There's nothing like taking a few moments to look out over the view and just remember how small you are in the scheme of things. It helps to relax me."

"Have you seen the view over Vale Valley? Our town, which is small, looks amazing."

"No, I've never seen it."

"When the weather's good, I'll take you out there. It's a sight to witness."

"I look forward to it."

They finished their main course, and then onto dessert, which was some cream pie. She couldn't eat her portion, so at Chip's request, she fed him hers.

He was right. She really couldn't think of him as Rufus. He was a Chip. Just the thought made her smile, and she couldn't seem to stop.

"That smile looks wicked."

"It's not. I'm happy. Very, very happy." They shared a coffee to finish the meal, and the waiter brought the check.

"How much?" she asked.

"This is my treat, and you don't have to worry about the cost." He pulled his card out, leaving it on the tray. Every now and then she saw the ink peeking out of the jacket that covered his arms.

She knew his arms were completely covered in pictures of death and destruction. Considering he seemed so level-headed and nice, the ink work was out of place, or at least to her it was.

Once they were finished, he escorted her out to the car, and they headed back toward town. Kasey lived on the other side, on the outskirts of Vale Valley in the town over.

Chip pulled into a parking bay and turned off the car.

"What is it?" she asked.

He tapped his fingers on the steering wheel and turned toward her. "Pie is going to try and date you as well."

"Oh, you know we only had lunch."

"He wants to date you, and I like you, Kasey. A lot."

"I like you, too."

"I was wondering if you were doing anything Sunday?" he asked.

She shook her head. "No, nothing."

"Would you like to hang out at the clubhouse with me? Watch a movie or something."

"Erm, sure. Do you not live elsewhere?"

"No, I don't. I've looked at other places but never felt the need to. Saving money up for when I needed it."

She nodded.

Kasey had been to the clubhouse a couple of times. The funeral was one time, and the other was when Strawberry fell down, banging her head. She'd checked her over.

"Are you sure I'm allowed to be there?"

"I've invited you. You can be anywhere you want to be."

Biting her lip, Kasey didn't want to jump ahead, but she also didn't want him to be under any wrong impression. "I'm not going to have sex with you." She slapped a hand over her mouth. "I didn't mean that the way it sounded. What I mean is, I can't just have sex and get over it."

He laughed. "I'm sorry. I'm not laughing even though I am. I'm not inviting you over for sex, Kasey. Don't get me wrong, I want to fuck you, have sex, make love. See, I'm just as bad at this. I'm used to being blunt."

"You can call it what you want, and be blunt. Don't ever change to please me." She reached out taking his hand. "I'm … new at all this dating, and I think I'm getting it wrong."

He shook his head. "I actually think you're getting it right. Sunday?"

"Call it a date."

Staring at him in the close confines of the car, she saw him look at her lips, and then begin to lean over. She knew he was going to kiss her, but she didn't once try to stop him.

The feel of his lips on hers sent a flood of desire straight between her thighs. Cupping his cheek, she kissed him back, melting as he held her close.

"You're so incredibly beautiful," he said.

****

Entering the clubhouse later that night, Chip was

on cloud nine, so fucking ecstatic. Kasey had agreed to another date, and as he took a seat he glanced over at the pool table where Landon had one of the club pussies bent over, and was taking her up the ass.

"How was the date?" Pie asked, grabbing a chair, spinning it around to straddle the main seat.

"Good. Really good. She likes Italian food." Since Pie wanted to date Kasey as well, he didn't want to give anything away. "I'm seeing her again on Sunday."

"You're not wasting any time, are you? Running from one date to another," Pie said.

"I like her."

"So do I."

He stared at Pie, who was glancing over his shoulder at the woman being fucked in the ass.

"You have a go at her?" Chip asked.

Pie returned his attention to him.

Chip held his hands up. "I'm not going to stop you from having at her. You seem to clearly want her."

"What's your game?" Pie asked.

"I'm not playing a single game right now." Chip nodded at Landon and the woman, whose name he really couldn't remember. "Are you wanting Kasey because I'm wanting her?"

"I like her."

"Yeah, but that doesn't mean you don't want club pussy either."

"You're telling me you don't want a taste of that tight ass that Landon has stretching out for any brother to want. She's stroking her clit, begging for another brother to slide into her mouth."

Chip shook his head. "I've not had a woman in months. Not interested in dipping my dick in anything else. I like Kasey." He had for a long time.

All he'd done was keep his thoughts and feelings

to himself. With everything going on, he didn't have time to talk to any of the brothers about settling down. Duke, Pike, Raoul, Crazy, Daisy, Knuckles, and Brass had all settled down. Each of the brothers had been spending more time at home than at the clubhouse especially with the Abelli threat. Since Anton Abelli had killed Russ and Sheila, and Duke had taken out Anton with the agreement that Francis was to leave them alone, it had been tense.

He wouldn't put it past Duke to start a war with the Abelli mafia. The brother was a maniac when it came to his woman, and anyone who posed a threat or stood in his way, needed to get the fuck out of it, or he'd take you down.

Pie stood up. "I'm bored of this shit."

Chip watched Pie walk away. It just so happened to be at the time Landon finished. He watched Pie grab the woman, hike her up onto his shoulder, and take her out of the room.

Bertie came to take a seat with him. It had been a while since Chip had spoken with the other club brother, who always remained a bit of a mystery. He didn't talk all that much, never had the need to.

Landon dropped down with a big, dramatic sigh. "I needed that, man. I tell you. All this tension has me worked up, and all I want to do is fuck. If you ask me it's why the brothers are keeping their old ladies at home. Worried about the competition."

"Roses were delivered to Holly at the ranch today," Bertie said.

Whatever joke Landon had been about to say died.

"Who from?" Chip asked, accepting the beer that Floss had brought over.

"Abelli, who else. Wants to talk."

"Maya got one as well," Landon said. "She tossed hers in the trashcan outside, and set them alight."

"We not going with the name Winter now?" Chip asked.

"No point. Everyone knows who she is, and she's under club protection."

Chip glanced around. "Where is she?"

"My room. She's studying for a chem test. Matthew's helping her."

Matthew was Duke's son, who'd been studying at home rather than going off to college.

"What's Duke said?" Chip asked.

"The moment he heard the news, he left the clubhouse. Didn't stick around. We've not seen him," Bertie said.

"So Abelli wants to talk."

"Holly's his grandkid, with their kids being his great-grandkids," Floss said.

"It doesn't matter. His son took out her parents, and Holly is really struggling with it," Landon said. "I heard Mary talking to Leanna the other day. Holly's taken the kids out of daycare, and has been homeschooling them."

"No shit!" Chip was surprised by that. Holly had been the one that wanted Matthew to venture out away from the club, to find a life that was his choice, and not one he felt he had to follow.

Duke had asked them all to treat him like a real Prospect. To give him a crash course in what was expected of all the new recruits. None of them had held anything back. Chip hadn't, making Matthew clean the shitty toilets, the laundry, and even cleaning up the main clubhouse after a serious fuck fest with lots of used condoms.

He'd not participated in the party, but he'd been

the brother to give the instruction to clean it up. He'd not seen Matthew around for a long time. The kid had decided to pick college rather than be a Prospect.

The club life wasn't for everyone, and Matthew had grown up to be a little punk ass. Some of the club had babysat that little kid, so none of them were willing to take his shit or his attitude.

"If Abelli wants to talk that means church is going to be called soon. Duke won't let this slide," Chip said.

"I know. Maya's not happy. She just wants to get on with her life," Landon said. "I can't blame her. After everything she's been through, the fact she can study shit like chemistry amazes me."

Landon had been put on Maya Abelli's protection detail. She'd been raped, beaten, and left for dead at the order of her own father. She was Holly's half-sister, and even that brought some complications. Some of the brothers had been worried that Landon was falling for the girl. He wasn't. Landon cared for Maya just like he did Zoe, Raoul's old lady. There was no love there. He saw Maya and Zoe as sisters.

"If this turns into a war, there's going to be a lot of casualties. Mafia against MC, it's not going to turn out great for either side," Bertie said.

Chip saw the somber looks on every single club brother. This was the tension hanging over the club.

What happened between Duke and Francis would determine their outcome.

They were each at a stalemate, but with the flowers being delivered with the request to talk, that had added something to the mix.

The game had started.

"Anyone remember when we just had a lot of fun?" Chip asked, wanting the guys to perk up a little.

"Remember when Duke had to chase after Holly because she wouldn't give him the time of day?" Floss said.

"I like Raoul, actually. That fucker was so scared that Duke was going to end him," Landon said.

Raoul had been the brother that took Holly to prom. He'd taken her virginity and pretty much dumped her ass.

Now *that* had caused some trouble in the club. Everything had been resolved with Holly and Raoul even being friends.

Time healed all wounds.

Chip finished his drink, listening to the brothers' stories, loving each memory as they came to him.

He'd been part of the club for most of his life, and he wouldn't change it for the world. From the age of eighteen, he'd wanted to be part of the Trojans MC, the badass group at the time run by Russ before it was given to Duke.

That was such a long time ago. He was thirty-nine years old. Then he couldn't help but smile. He'd finally experienced his first date at thirty-nine years old, and it had been the best night of his life.

Calling it a night first, he left the brothers to drink, and talk. He wanted to be alone to think about the ramifications of what was going to happen if Abelli didn't step down.

Chapter Four

Holly stared at the flowers and didn't know what to do. Duke wanted to throw them in the trash, and she just kept staring at them. They were a mixture of white and red roses, an elaborate and beautiful display, so big they must have cost a fortune.

Matthew had put the kids to bed as she simply stared at the flowers. Tucking her hair behind her ears, she knew she had to get it cut soon as it had grown too long, and she was finding it harder to deal with.

"Tell me what you're thinking, baby," Duke said, wrapping his arms around her waist, and pulling her close. He kissed her head, and she closed her eyes.

He was so worried about her.

Right now, she was struggling. She wouldn't lie. The thought of going outside and being part of the club terrified her.

Her parents, all three of them, were gone.

Taken from her by a madman. Her mother killed. Russ, her stepfather, dead. Even Anton Abelli was gone. The crazy assed loser who'd ruined her life.

Biting her lip, she grabbed hold of Duke's arm, and he held her close.

"Hold me, Duke."

"I'm holding you, babe. I won't let go."

She took several deep breaths, refusing to allow the tears to fall. Vale Valley had been her home for so long. She couldn't even remember her life outside of it, and she didn't want to.

This was just … a nightmare.

"Maya got one as well."

She closed her eyes and took another breath. The anger she felt consumed every single part of her.

"They're settled," Matthew said, appearing in front of her. He held his hands up. "Sorry. I'll head to my room. Get some studying done."

He'd been a real blessing the past couple of days, and right now she wasn't behaving like a very good person.

"Thank you, Matt. You're amazing."

He winked. "Think about that when it comes to laundry day."

She chuckled.

Alone with Duke, she pulled away, and he cupped her face, stroking her cheeks. "Why won't you leave the house?"

"It hurts too much. Everywhere I go, I have memories. They're everywhere, and I can't … I'm not that strong."

"You're a strong woman, Holly. You've helped me raise my teenage son, and he's becoming a fine man. You're my old lady, and your mother taught you well."

A sob escaped.

"Everyone is missing you. Mary, Zoe, Pike, Landon, everyone. The whole club, and Mary's worried. Your blog, your world, don't let it fall apart because of this."

"I don't know what to do," she said, grabbing his shirt, and pressing her face against his chest.

"I know for a fact that Pie and several of the guys are eating at Mac's place. They can't stand the microwavable shit that's on offer. Mac and cheese from a box. We're better than that," Duke said.

"What happened to the other old ladies?"

"They come and go, but they have work as well. The club hasn't been the same since Russ and Sheila died. I hate to do this to you, babe, I know you need more time. I need you. The club needs you."

"Is he going to start a war?" Holly asked. "I don't think I can stand another death. Not now, not ever."

"No. I won't let it get to a war." He pulled her close, and she breathed a sigh of relief.

"Do you think that's what he wants?"

"For his sake, I hope not."

She knew Duke had killed Anton. His death had come at Duke's hand, and she didn't care. Anton had played a game, and taken her parents from her.

Pulling out of Duke's arms, she grabbed the vase of flowers and walked outside, tossing it straight into the trash.

****

Kasey bit her lip, wondering if she should continue up the drive or leave. Since her date last night with Chip, she'd been thinking about Holly, and wanted to do her a pie. She stayed up late last night baking the one her brother had made for her after their parents died, the one he always made for her when she felt ill or depressed.

He'd called it the "get-well-soon-pie": chocolate, caramel sauce, brownie, pie crust, and pudding.

Probably enough calories to sink a ship but still, one slice always made her feel better. Of course, once she finished the slice she felt sick, but that was the curse. One slice never was enough, at least not to her.

She tensed up as she saw a bike coming down the driveway. Duke stopped, and she pressed the button for her window to come down.

"Hey, Kasey," he said.

"Hey. Erm, I hope it's okay. I have a pie I made for Holly. Is it okay for me to go and see her? I know she's been through a lot."

"I'd really appreciate it, actually. I think I'm finally getting through to her." He nodded at her and took off. Making the final decision, Kasey drove down toward the ranch and climbed out of the car, reaching in for the pie as the front door opened.

"Kasey, what a nice surprise," Holly said.

When she turned to see Holly, Kasey was shocked. In the past month since her parents' death and funeral, Holly had lost a lot of weight.

"I hope you don't mind me crashing your time." She lifted up the pie. "I came with gifts."

"Gifts are always appreciated." Holly pulled her in for a hug, and Kasey tightened her arm around her, wanting to offer the other woman support.

"Come in. Come in."

Entering the large ranch, she saw Matthew sitting on the sofa while the kids watched television.

"I'll keep an eye on them," he said, giving her a wave.

Kasey waved back, and she followed Holly into the kitchen.

"I heard that you've been dating two of the Trojans MC," Holly said.

"Dating two? No, no, I've had lunch with Pie and dinner with Chip. I'm actually seeing him Sunday night. We're going to watch a movie, and I'm rambling. I need to stop rambling so much."

Holly chuckled. "It's nice to hear someone else talk for a change. I feel I spend way too much time with the kids."

"I wanted to give this to you. This was my brother's recipe. He believed that it cured every single ailment in the world."

"Does it work?" Holly asked.

"It helps. It doesn't cure everything, but it helps. He … made it after my parents died."

Holly tensed up. "I totally forgot that your parents

had died."

"A car accident. I was fifteen."

"Wow. So … young."

"I don't think it matters what age you lose them. It hurts, and yours died in really bad circumstances."

"My real father did the hit." Holly pressed her lips together. "I'm sorry."

"It's fine. I get it. You've probably had a lot of people tell you that they understand. I guess in a way I do. They were killed because of a drunk driver. I remember the anger, the rage. I wanted to hurt them. My brother kept me stable."

"Then you lost your brother."

"Yes, and again everything went to crap. Pardon my language."

"I live with a lot of badass bikers. Crap is a tame word."

"You've not been around the bikers though. Chip said that you've not been around as much." Kasey didn't know why she was talking and invading Holly's privacy like this. She didn't even know if she could help her. She only knew she had to try.

Holly finished making them both a coffee, and placed it in front of her, taking a seat at the table.

"The life I led, it wasn't the truth. My mom was on the run from my father, and the Trojans had such a hard reputation that Russ kept us all safe." Holly rubbed at her eyes. "The clubhouse was Russ's for so long. Every room holds a memory to me. I remember so much laughter, and then of course the lies." Holly averted her gaze. "The parking lot, where they were shot just outside the clubhouse."

"They're all memories."

"Every single one."

Kasey sat back, and thought about it. "I work in

Vale Valley hospital. My brother died in that hospital, in the emergency room where I work. I go inside there every single day. The pain at times gets less, but then there are times it only seems to get worse." She paused, watching Holly's reaction. "I even got to the store where he got shot. Our memories don't define who we are. Actions do." Her brother had been shot outside of a store. It was a random shooting that he'd gotten in the middle of. She'd never forget the phone conversation, or that incredible feeling of loneliness after he died.

"I don't feel strong enough."

"You're a mother, Holly. You're a strong woman. You've just got to realize how strong."

Tears filled Holly's eyes, and without waiting, Kasey was out of her seat and holding onto the other woman. "It's fine for you to hide, but you can't do it forever."

"Why are you helping me?"

"I was following your blog, and I've not cooked anything new that has worked in so long. I miss you and Mary. Please, please, please, help a woman out."

"You use our blog?"

"From the moment I first stumbled onto it. Your pictures have become a lot better, and clearer. Everything that you guys create works." She hugged Holly another time and stepped back. "Shall I cut you a slice of pie? It may work."

"Go on. I'd love to try it."

Finding a knife, Kasey cut two slices, putting one in front of Holly. She took a seat again, and watched as Holly took a bite. "This is good."

"A cure for most ills."

"You know, I'm so pleased you came today."

"You are?"

"Yes. Duke and I talked last night, and he told me

he needed me."

Kasey took another bite of the pie. "It should have come from someone else."

Holly shook her head. "No. Mary tried. As did Zoe, and Leanna, even my sister, Maya. They all tried, and I told them to get out." She blew out a breath. "Wow, I owe a lot of apologies."

"You still love to cook though, right?"

"I love it."

"Then I'd just do a big luxurious spread or something, and maybe throw in an apology," Kasey said.

"You think that would do the trick?"

"Yeah. I do." She'd seen the way the guys respected and cared for Holly. She was the queen in their world. "If you ever need to talk, I don't mind listening."

"Thank you, Kasey." Holly covered her mouth as chocolate drizzled down the corner of her mouth. "This is really good pie."

"My brother's cure."

"Can I use it on our blog? You will get total credit."

"No. Could you credit my brother?"

"Yes," Holly said.

"Then yes. When I get home, I'll write it down for you."

Finishing off her pie, Kasey stayed for another cup of coffee, and then she climbed into her car, heading home.

She hoped she'd helped Holly.

Loss was hard for everyone. Coping with that loss was also different, and she understood Holly's withdrawal. She'd done the same, only she'd wanted to turn to drugs, which she hadn't, in the end.

Life had a way of throwing you into paths you never thought you'd venture down. Kasey intended to help as many people as possible. It was one of the reasons she became a nurse.

****

The following day, Chip stood in the doorway of the kitchen and wondered if he'd entered the Twilight Zone or something.

The kitchen was spotless, and he knew last night it had been totally trashed with beer bottles everywhere.

"Am I seeing this right?" Floss asked.

"Damn, that's Holly?" Pie asked.

All of the guys were standing in the doorway as Holly whirled around to glare at them. "Seriously, I've been gone a short time and you guys can't even clean up after yourselves? I checked the laundry room. How do you guys even have clothes? There's piles mountain-high. Who's been in charge while I've been away?"

Everyone pointed at everyone else, and she tutted.

"I come here to make everyone Sunday lunch, and I've already had to call reinforcements with the other old ladies. I cannot cook in this kitchen." She put down the bag she'd been holding, and moved toward two large bags. "I have brisket. A pot roast all planned with lots of dressing, vegetables, the works, and I can't get it done with this mess." She held up a large brisket, and knowing Holly, there were at least three if not four that size.

It had been a long time since she cooked on a Sunday.

Just the thought of the food that could be coming their way made his mouth water.

She put the meat down and then grabbed the bag. "Ew, who had sex in the kitchen? This is just gross." She held up a used condom.

"I suggest you boys get to work," Duke said. They turned to see him holding Bell, and he had a huge smile on his face. They had all been missing Holly, but none more so than Duke. "You want Sunday lunch, it's time to start acting like you give a shit about this place."

No one complained as they all got started in cleaning up the clubhouse, opening up windows and cleaning the place.

"She's back! I'm so getting my burgers and pies," Pie said.

Chip couldn't help but smile as he made his way into the kitchen wearing a pair of pink gloves to get cleaning.

"Where do you need me to start?" he asked.

"Cleaning the dishes. This place is just a mess. I had no idea it had gotten this bad, and I'm ashamed of myself for not checking on you guys sooner. This will not happen again."

She picked up all the beer cans and bottles, along with wrappings.

"It's good to have you back, Holly."

"It's good to be back, actually. You should thank Kasey. That woman is a keeper."

Chip looked toward her. "Kasey?"

"She came to visit me. We talked. I think she was nervous talking about her life. She's lost so much, and she wanted to tell me that she understood, and that if I ever needed anyone to talk to, I wasn't alone."

"You're not alone," Chip said.

"She strikes me as being a keeper. Do I sense something like that between you two?" she asked.

"I like her a lot."

"Pie's also making a pitch for her," Holly said.

He shrugged. "I'm not worried."

Pie wasn't really interested in winning over Kasey. Chip had no doubt that the brother probably fancied her, and maybe even wanted to fuck her, but the difference between him and Pie was that he wanted forever, not just a bit of fun.

They got back to working, scrubbing the kitchen until it had a nice shine to it. The other old ladies arrived, and it wasn't long before the clubhouse was back to its former self.

"You did it," Chip said, putting his arm around her shoulder, and giving her arm a squeeze.

"I think my mother would be proud," Holly said.

He knew she hurt just saying that. "She would be."

Just then the kitchen door opened, and the woman Pie had taken from Landon came in. "Wow, this place sure cleans up nicely. You're damn good at your job."

Chip watched as she brushed past them, heading for the coffee.

"Do you know if the Prez is serious with his wife?"

Holly tensed up, and Chip realized the sweet-butt didn't have a clue who Holly was.

"Duke's into his wife, all right."

The sweet-butt glared at Holly. "Wasn't talking to you. Why don't you go and clean something? Everything needs to be cleaned after all." She turned her smile to Chip, but he wasn't impressed.

Before he could do anything, Holly stepped forward. "You better watch your mouth. I'm Duke's old lady. *I'm* his woman. I wear his patch, I'm by his side. Don't think for a second for making a play for my man, or I will show you how an old lady deals with a person like you."

"Get gone," Chip said.

Holly shook from the rage.

"You okay, momma bear?"

"Have I really been gone that long the women don't know me?" Holly asked.

"That's why I know I've not got a problem with Pie. She screwed Landon and Pie last night. I'll let the boys know to keep an eye out. She looked like she was after a patch."

Holly took a deep breath. "I've got to get started on lunch. I don't even want to know what is going on."

Chip left her to it. He didn't cook anything other than heating up cans of premade chili.

Heading outside for some fresh air and to get ready to go and pick Kasey up, he found Duke pulling out some bags of shopping from the back of the car.

"It's good to see her back."

"Whatever Kasey did, tell her thank you," Duke said. "I talked to Holly, and I think I got through. But Kasey helped, I'm sure of it."

"Kasey's lost everyone. I have no doubt she said something that struck a chord with Holly."

Duke nodded, rubbing at his eyes. "It has been a long few weeks."

"Still, she's back, and she's cooking. The brothers look happy about that. Oh, Holly's just had a run in with a new sweet-butt."

Duke groaned. "Why do I feel I'm not going to like this shit?"

"You're not. She thought Holly was a cleaner. I would have called cat fight, but you know I like to keep that shit to myself. Warn the brothers, though. I think that woman is trying to find herself a patch. Do what Crazy's ex did on him."

Crazy's ex, who was dead, had trapped him into marriage by getting pregnant. Of course, his ex hadn't given a shit about the kid, and it had driven Crazy mad being attached to the bitch.

Chip vowed never to fall for any of the tricks the club whores might try to play. He liked his life exactly the way it was.

Of course, now he hoped that Kasey would like to join in that life with him.

Chapter Five

"You're telling me nothing sexy happened?" Lindsey asked.

"Nothing sexy. Nothing bad. We had a lot of fun." Kasey laughed as she flipped another pancake. She didn't have much choice in making them as Lindsey brought them 'round with her, and pretty much begged for her to cook them.

She didn't mind cooking.

"This is so not fair. I bet he'd be amazing in the sack. Those big hands running all over your body, squeezing your tits, and ass, holding you still as he drove inside you." Lindsey groaned. "My date so didn't pan out."

"Are you a sex addict?"

"Nah, maybe, I'm not sure. I can go without sex for a long time, and I'm not like desperate or anything, but you know how it is. Sometimes you just need to have a really good fuck."

Kasey didn't dispute her neighbor, even though she couldn't agree with her either.

"Oh my God, are you telling me right now that you don't have a clue what I'm talking about?" Lindsey asked.

"Of course I do."

"No. You see, Kasey, I know you, and that face right there is not a face of someone who gets what I'm saying. Have you even had sex before?"

"Of course I have."

"When?" Lindsey asked. "When was the last time you had sex?"

"A long time ago. It didn't work out." She shrugged, not wanting to make it a big deal.

"How can … do you even own a vibrator?"

"Please, Lindsey, enough. I can't just have sex with a guy I've just met."

"Why not?" Lindsey asked. "Most guys can screw a woman on the first ten minutes of meeting."

"I'm not comfortable getting naked with some guy."

"Why not? You're hot. I'd totally do you right now if you'd like."

"Stop doing that. I know you're all liberated, and stuff, but I'm not like that. I like you as a friend, and we will never go that far," Kasey said.

Lindsey held her hands up. "Fine, fine. I'm just saying like it is."

"I've never been … filled with that need to get naked and have hot, sweaty sex with a guy." Even though Chip certainly got her worked up.

Late last night her body had been on fire, and she'd thought about him as she touched herself. She'd brought herself to orgasm just thinking of Chip's hands all over her body, his cock driving inside her, and she had loved every single second of it.

"I'm so sorry. I didn't mean to make you feel uncomfortable. I'm all about expressing myself. I don't have that filter that everyone seems to possess."

"It's fine," Kasey said.

She left the counter and gave Lindsey a very friends-only hug.

Making her way back toward the kitchen, she flipped the pancakes just as the doorbell rang.

"I'll get that."

Kasey didn't know who it would be, but when she heard Chip's voice, her heart fluttered. Her pussy came alive and her nipples tightened.

She'd never had such an instant reaction before,

and she hoped the padded bra she wore wouldn't show him how aroused his voice made her.

"Well, well, well, my day just got all shiny," Lindsey said. "Chip's here to see you."

She watched as Lindsey took a seat.

Her neighbor had admitted to her many months ago that even though she didn't mind expressing herself, men in relationships were completely, one hundred percent, off limits to her. She didn't screw guys with rings.

Chip held a single rose in his hand.

"You don't have to constantly bring gifts. You could just bring yourself. I wouldn't have a problem with that."

He handed her the rose and took her hand, placing a kiss on her knuckles. She recalled the kiss in the car, and wished Lindsey weren't there so she could sneak another kiss in.

"It's a thank you," he said.

"What for?"

"Talking to Holly."

"You know I talked to her?"

"I woke up and found her cleaning up the kitchen. She had everything ready to prepare Sunday lunch, and that is not something I've seen in a long time."

"Then I'm pleased I was able to help." She smiled, thinking about Holly.

"You talked to her."

"I did. She wasn't in the best place, and sometimes it can take someone saying that feeling certain things is okay."

"You're not going to tell me what they are?"

"Patient-client privilege. You've got your secrets. I have mine." She smiled as he reached out and tucked a curl behind her ear.

She always put her hair up, but after their date, she suddenly liked wearing it down.

"So, the club is having Sunday lunch, and I figured seeing as you helped with everything, it's only fair that I invite you. I've got some movies, lots of chips and dips."

"You're going out?" Lindsey asked.

"You didn't give me the chance to tell you that I'm heading out this evening. Spending time with Chip." She put her arm around him, and Lindsey seemed to melt.

"You two make like the cutest couple in the world. I just adore seeing you both together." Lindsey grabbed her cell phone. "I've so got to take a picture."

She snapped the photos using her phone, and Kasey pulled away after several shots to grab the pancakes.

Lindsey showed her the pictures. "You could end your fasting with him. He knows what he's doing."

"And he can probably hear you, so shhh."

"Can I join for pancakes?" Chip asked.

"If you'd like some. I made plenty."

Taking a seat between Chip and Lindsey, she glanced at him to see if he showed any signs of overhearing Lindsey's words. She couldn't see anything.

Cutting into her pancake, she drizzled a little more maple syrup over hers as she liked them incredibly sweet. She didn't have any room for savory when it came to pancakes.

"I was hoping to invite you to dinner," Chip said. "Holly's cooking. The gang's back together, and I want you to see what you've done."

Kasey finished chewing her mouthful, and looked toward him. "Is that allowed?"

He burst out laughing. "It's a biker club, babe.

Not a jail. Of course, you're free to come as well." He looked toward Lindsey.

Her neighbor held her hand up. "That's okay. You and Kasey have a great time."

"It's not trouble if you want to join us. I know a guy I'd like to introduce you to." Kasey saw her friend's interest perk right up.

"Now you have my full attention."

"You can come for dinner, and we'll drive you back. It's no trouble."

Lindsey looked toward her. "Would you mind me crashing with you?"

"It doesn't bother me."

"Yay. I totally have to change."

Before anyone could say anything, Lindsey was out of the door, and Kasey laughed at her retreating figure.

"You don't mind me inviting her?" he asked.

"Of course not. She wants to go to the clubhouse, and has been asking me constant questions about it."

"So, what fasting are we talking about here?"

She looked toward Chip and saw him smiling. "You heard that?"

"Lindsey can't whisper at all. I heard every single word."

"Ugh." She groaned, rubbing at her forehead. "Please, ignore her. She doesn't know what she's talking about half the time."

He chuckled. "I don't mind."

Their breakfast finished, Kasey grabbed the plates and headed into her small kitchen. Placing them in the sink, she felt Chip move up behind her.

She turned to face him, and wished for a split second that she hadn't done that. He was so close, and his breath fanned her face.

Licking her dry lips, she stared up at him. His green eyes captured her, holding her steady, as he stepped a little closer.

"What kind of fasting?" He pushed some of her hair back, and her body tensed up, not in fear, but in arousal.

"It's nothing."

"Doesn't sound like nothing."

"I've not been with a man in a really long time. That's the kind of fasting she's talking about. Sex."

"Now how has a gorgeous girl like yourself gotten away without fucking?"

His bluntness shocked her. She liked it even. He didn't try to evade anything. He always said what was on his mind, and she liked that more than anything. She hated when people were vague or holding back the truth.

"I'm ... sex means something to me. It has to. Guys tend to want to take me to visit their parents, and sex always is the last thing on their mind." She'd never been wowed by a guy before, not until Chip came along at least.

In the past couple of days, he'd certainly inspired a lot of feelings from her, but none of them about love, at least not yet.

He aroused her.

Her dreams were heavily dominated by him, and what his hands and tongue could do to her body.

"Have you ever thought that you've not found the right guy to fuck?" he asked.

"I don't know."

He cupped her cheek, tilting her head back, and she saw the smile in his gaze. "Your body is giving away your response, baby."

"What?"

"Your nipples are tight, and your eyes are saying

'take me now.'" The sound of a door slamming had Chip pulling away. "I think we'll explore that later."

Lindsey was already back, and Kasey gritted her teeth. Need had rushed right through her, and she craved his touch unlike anything else in the world.

****

Blue balls.

Chip was convinced if he took the time to look at his dick and balls, they would be blue, and the tip of his cock weeping with pre-cum. Glancing over at Kasey, he wished they were alone and he could get his hands on her.

Hearing Lindsey coming back had really messed with his plans. He'd intended to press Kasey up against the kitchen counter, remove those tight jeans, and taste her pretty pussy. Moving a little in his seat to relieve the ache, he focused on the road, getting them back to the clubhouse.

"I cannot wait to go inside the club. It has always been a dream of mine to see inside one. I bet it totally rocks, and all you guys are so hot," Lindsey said.

"What do you do for a living, Lindsey?" he asked.

"I'm a receptionist at a plastic surgery clinic."

He glanced up in the rearview mirror, and saw her roll her eyes. "I know. It is such a shit, crappy job. The people that come in often leave in tears." She shrugged. "They're there to tell everyone they're not pretty. It pays really good money, and I only have to work five days a week, so yay me. I won't do it forever, though. Nope."

"Sounds like an interesting job."

"Not really. It's boring as fuck. Not only that, three of the surgeons have come up to me, and told me that even though I'm stunning, they can make me even better. I told them to stick their scalpel up their ass and fuck themselves."

Kasey burst out laughing. "Oh, my, and you still have a job?"

"Of course. You see, the key to working in such a shitty environment like that is to be, like, super-confident with yourself. Me, I love the way I look. I'm not being vain, but I have no intention of ever, ever getting beneath a scalpel. They can kiss my ass before I'd even consider doing anything like that," Lindsey said.

"I can't believe you'd be so blunt."

"Meh, in this world you've got to be. Isn't your club about living to your own set of rules and totally saying screw it to everyone else?"

"I get what you're saying."

"Exactly. I have no interest in being a perfect, plastic woman. If a guy doesn't like me for how I look now, then screw them. In fifty years, unless my genes have been really good to me, I'm not going to look this great. That's the thing. I'm looking for my forever guy just as I'm enjoying having some fun."

Chip reached out and squeezed Kasey's knee.

Lindsey kept on talking, and he looked at Kasey, who was smiling back at him.

In no time at all, they were arriving back at the clubhouse, and Lindsey's excitement reached fever pitch as he parked the car.

As he was climbing out, Lindsey was already bouncing where she stood.

Kasey came to his side, and he wrapped an arm around her waist. If his plan worked, Pie would be completely smitten with Lindsey, and any competition Chip faced would be finished with. Not that he minded the competition at all. He wanted Kasey all to himself.

As they headed inside the very clean clubhouse,

the sounds of laughter, children's playful screams, and chatter filled the air. Already a large table was set for dinner, and the scents made his mouth water.

"It smells amazing," she said.

The aroma of beef filled the air.

Duke had Bell in his arms, and he made his way over toward them. "Thank you."

"You don't need to thank me for anything."

"Whatever you said or did, it brought her back, and I know I may have helped with that, but you gave her the final push."

"I'm pleased that she's back."

Even Chip loved how the clubhouse finally felt. For too long it had felt like a ghost house, the energy having died when Russ and Sheila were taken from them.

"If there's ever anything you need at any time, you call me, and the club will have your back."

"Thank you."

Duke moved on, and Kasey breathed a sigh of relief. "He can be quite scary."

Chip was used to seeing Duke smitten with his kids and woman, but he'd also seen him commit murder without even blinking, washing blood from his hands as if it was just mud from the garden.

To a lot of people, he imagined Duke was a force to be reckoned with. "I think you're safe. He's in your debt."

"Let's hope I'm never in his."

Just then Pie came out of a room, and Chip noticed him pushing his shirt back into his pants, and the girl that had been trying to put Holly in her place came out after him. Her lipstick was smeared.

The moment Pie saw Kasey, he came on over.

Holding her waist, Chip pulled her a little closer. The sweet-butt came along with him.

"Kasey, I had no idea you were coming."

"Sweetie, you've got something wrong with your lipstick," Lindsey said, coming out from behind them.

On the way inside, Lindsey had gotten a text or something, and she'd been clicking away while Duke had been talking to them.

"Sorry, just keeping my man occupied."

"Lindsey, I'd like you to meet Pie," Chip said.

"Holy crap. You're the guy with the flowers." Lindsey's arms folded, and Chip had read her right.

For all of her bubbly personality, her loyalty to Kasey was that of a best friend. He wondered if his woman even realized that she'd gotten a friend for life in Lindsey.

"What are you doing giving flowers to one woman and getting your dick sucked from another?" Lindsey had also stepped a little in front of Kasey, protecting her.

"Lindsey, it's fine, really."

"You see, I don't think it is. I don't think it's funny or fair at all."

"Kasey, it's so good to see you here."

"Hey, Pie. Was that your girlfriend? You didn't say you had a girlfriend."

"She's not my girlfriend. She's, erm…"

"Kasey!" Holly came rushing out of the kitchen, and Chip stepped back as Kasey was pulled into a hug. "I'm so pleased you came. I had no idea you were invited, and I don't have your number, and I've been waiting for Crazy to pass it to me."

"Chip came and invited me to dinner. Also, we brought my very … boisterous neighbor. Lindsey, I'd like you to meet Holly. She's Duke's old lady."

"Now it is a pleasure to meet you." Lindsey pulled Holly in for a hug. "I've always wanted to come to a clubhouse, and this place does not disappoint."

"On a Sunday it's a little more to do with family than partying."

Pie glared at him.

"I'm going to grab something to drink. Want a soda?" Chip asked.

Lindsey and Kasey both nodded. He left his woman with Holly, knowing it wouldn't be long before the other old ladies descended on them. Entering the kitchen, Pie followed him.

"What game are you playing?" Pie asked.

"I'm not playing any game. Do you like her neighbor?" He'd also misjudged Lindsey. She didn't seem interested in Pie at all. Fine, fine, he could handle that. At the end of the day, so long as Pie realized he didn't stand a chance with Kasey, he was happy.

"Why did you bring her here?"

Chip grabbed three sodas out of the fridge, and turned to give the brother his full attention. "In case your face has been shoved so far up that slut's pussy, let me remind you. I want Kasey. I'm dating Kasey. She's mine. I invited her over tonight to watch a movie, and she helped Holly to get her back to the clubhouse. We can argue about this, or you can get over whatever shit you think is going on."

Pie rubbed the back of his head. "I thought she was the one."

"If you think a woman is the one, you don't put your dick in another hole." He shrugged. "We good?"

Duke wouldn't be in the mood for any of them to be fighting with each other.

"Yeah, we're good."

Pie left him alone, and taking the sodas out to the women, Chip saw Kasey and Lindsey were both having a good time. He gave a soda to Lindsey and stayed with

Kasey, handing her a soda then opening up his own.

With Kasey at the clubhouse and knowing Pie was taking a step back, he felt … better.

Chapter Six

Kasey had been talking a lot with Landon and Maya throughout the evening. Later that night, after they'd dropped Lindsey back home, Chip took them both back to the clubhouse, and after grabbing some snacks, they made their way toward his bedroom.

On the way to the stairs that led up to the rooms, she paused when she caught sight of Pie, fucking a woman who was bent over a pool table. A couple of the men were watching, and the sight fired Kasey's blood, shocking her.

Not because it was Pie screwing a woman but the act itself, the raw need that was showing between the two people.

She'd never had that.

"Do you like Pie?" Chip asked.

Smiling back at Chip, she nodded. "He's nice. He's fun to talk to."

Chip looked back over at Pie. "Do you wish you were her right now?"

"What? No, ew. I actually consider Pie just a friend, really. He's easy to talk to, and he doesn't demand a lot of … energy. I don't have a crush or feelings for Pie." She saw Chip relax a little more. "Did you think I did?"

"I don't know. Pie wanted to make you his."

"He did?"

"The flowers."

"That's what those were for? I thought he was just being friendly." Her cheeks were heating. "They were just a bunch of flowers, and it even had the cost sticker attached. Like last-minute deliveries or something."

"I don't just want to be your friend," Chip said.

He took her hand, leading her up to his room. She watched as he closed and locked the door. Sitting down on the edge of his bed, she waited for him.

"I've wanted you for a long time, Kasey."

"You have? You've not said anything."

He turned toward her and took a seat beside her. He held her hand, and she locked her fingers with his, enjoying his close contact. It felt good to be near him, to be close. Resting her head on his shoulder, she smiled.

"I was teasing," she said.

"What?"

She chuckled. "This couldn't be any more awkward if we tried. I know you like me, Chip. I know you want to date me, and I also want to date you." She stared up at him. "Can I be honest with you?"

"About everything. You don't have to hold anything back."

"I've never felt anything like that downstairs."

"What do you mean?"

"Sex. I've … it has always been so mechanical, and I've never … you know. Wow, I'm a thirty-year-old nurse, and I can't even say it."

"You've never had a guy bend you over, and fuck you so hard because he couldn't resist for another second not doing it?"

She sighed. "You make it sound so perfect."

He chuckled. "It can be so perfect, Kasey. There's been many a surface I've wanted to just fuck you on. Of course, I've not done that. I don't want you to think I'm hurting you. I want you. I hope you have no doubt about that."

Placing his hand at her knee, he began to slide it up and down.

She stared at his hand. Her pussy was already

wet, now even more so just from his touch alone. He made her ache.

Taking hold of his hand, she locked their fingers together, wanting his touch.

"I don't know what to say or do half the time," she said. "Dating. This, whatever it is, I don't … I'm not used to any of this."

He cupped her cheek, tilting her head back so that she looked into his green eyes. "Why don't we take it one step at a time? Don't plan anything. You're my woman, and I'm your man."

"Exclusive?"

"I won't step out on you. I won't fuck this up, and we'll go at your pace. I'm not in a rush. I want to take my time. Get to know you, and for you to get accustomed to me."

The way he looked at her, the hunger in his gaze—unable to resist for even a moment longer, she held the back of his head, and pulled him down to kiss.

The moment his lips touched her, her nipples beaded and she released a little moan, needing more, needing him.

He stroked her cheek at the same time she teased her tongue across his lips. When he opened his mouth, she plunged in, tasting him.

Her pussy was on fire with the need to touch, but she didn't take it any further than kissing him.

"I only have so much control," he said, pulling away.

"What?"

He took her hand, placing it over his dick. "This is what you do to me. I can only take so much."

She squeezed his cock, and feeling a little more brazen, she placed his hand over her pussy, the jeans she wore offering another layer of protection. Taking his lips once again, she kissed him as she rubbed his cock.

The palm of his hand pressed between her thighs, and she gasped as he pressed the seam of her jeans between her slit. The panties she wore just seemed to get in the way, but every single nerve ending seemed to catch a light with the barest touch of his palm no matter the number of clothes she wore.

"I bet you're soaking wet for me."

"Yes."

"I want to taste you. I want to strip you naked and kiss every single inch of your body right now."

Pulling back a little, Kasey bit her lip. She wanted that, too, but it had only been a couple of dates.

All of her life, apart from her little delve into darkness, she'd waited, she'd done the right thing. Even when dates had been going better than she thought they were, she'd wanted things to progress, but the men she'd been with had always held back.

She no longer wanted to hold back.

Standing up, she stepped in front of him, meeting his gaze.

"Do you want me?"

"More than anything else in the world."

Nodding her head, she liked his answer. Slowly, she began to open the buttons of her shirt.

Staring into his eyes, she didn't lose her nerve as his gaze followed the direction. That morning, after waking from a very good, very explicit dream, she'd dressed in a sexy red lacy lingerie set.

Removing her shirt, she let it drop to the floor.

"Fuck me," he said.

He stood up, and she watched him remove his leather cut, followed by his shirt, which he tugged over his head.

Reaching behind her, she unsnapped the button,

and slowly dropped the bra to the floor.

Chip put his hand on her waist and pulled her closer.

"You look utterly breathtaking," he said.

The hand on her waist moved up to cup her breast. The moment he grazed her hard nipple, it sent another wave of pleasure straight to her core.

Putting her hands on his shoulders, she stared into his eyes once again, feeling herself getting lost in his embrace.

"You're a lot taller than I am," she said, chuckling.

He laughed, bending down and taking her lips.

Sliding her hands down his body, she fingered the belt holding his jeans up. She loved the look of his ass in jeans, and a couple of times that she'd seen him, she'd admired him. The tux had looked sexy as hell, but nowhere near as good as his jeans.

As she opened his belt, Chip did the same with her jeans. Within seconds they were both naked as he took her panties with him.

His boxer briefs were the only things he wore. The hard outline of his dick pressed against the front, and she reached out, touching him.

He gripped her ass, pulling her closer, and she gasped once again.

Chip took charge, dropping her to the bed, and she spread her thighs to make room for him.

"It's like you were made for me and me alone," he said, taking her lips as he kissed her. The fire between her legs built, and she wanted his cock.

She wanted him to fuck her, to take her, and to make her his.

He broke from the kiss, and began to trail his lips down her body, going to one breast then the other, and back again to take a nipple into his mouth.

She cried out as he bit down. The pain mixed with pleasure, making it impossible for her to concentrate on anything else as he drove her wild with need.

He licked, sucked, kissed down her body, dipping into her belly button before he rested just above her pussy.

Moving up to her elbows, she spread her thighs wide.

"You're so wet already."

Heat flooded her cheeks.

"I love that. I love how wet you are. Has anyone ever taken the time to love this body?"

She shook her head.

"No one ever tasted this pretty cunt?"

Again, she shook her head.

He groaned.

Chip spread the lips of her pussy, opening her up, and she gasped as he slid his tongue between her slit, touching her clit, then going down to her entrance, and he circled her pussy before sliding inside.

She cried out his name as the pleasure rushed forward.

It was unlike anything she'd ever felt.

The feel of his tongue was pure rapture, and she couldn't look away nor did she want to.

Chip held her completely at his mercy.

****

The kids were asleep in their room in the clubhouse. Standing in the doorway of the kitchen, Duke watched as Holly finished wiping down the table. The dinner had been a raving success, and Mary used the time to take snaps. He'd already gotten the alert on his phone about a new post from his wife's blog.

Yes, he followed her cooking blog. He loved to

see what new creations she made, and there were times the club, and work within the club, took him away.

He'd never intended to fall in love with Holly. There was an age gap between them, but their differences hadn't mattered. He'd wanted her, fallen in love with her, and her troubles were his, and vice versa.

She moved toward the kitchen sink, and he made his way up behind her, wrapping his arms around her waist, and kissing her neck. She sighed, leaning against him.

"Hey," she said.

"You're the only one still here, and I don't think you can make this room any cleaner. They could do surgery the place is that clean."

"It wasn't when I came in. The place was disgusting." She shuddered.

"I've been so busy with everything else, the cleanliness of the club seemed to be bottom of the list," he said.

Every night he'd wanted to get home, to help Holly, to be there for his family while she struggled.

When she withdrew from Mary, and he'd been informed that she'd told everyone to get the fuck out of their house, he'd known he was in trouble. Mary and Holly were the best of friends, the kind of friendship where they could speak the truth and still be friends afterward. Mary had warned him that Holly was in a dark place, and he needed to get her out of it.

"It was good to see Mary. I apologized. The last time I saw her, I was a bitch to her, and everyone else at the club. I think Pie wanted to kiss my feet."

Her food and Mary's had always gotten a rave response at the club.

"This is your place, Hols. Always has been, and always will be."

She hugged him back, and he closed his eyes, grateful that his wife was back.

"Do you think he's going to hurt the club?"

"Francis?"

"Yeah."

"I won't let him hurt the club."

"I don't want him sending flowers, or trying to make a connection. I'm done. Russ was my father, and I didn't get the chance to tell him that before he died. I was so angry with him."

"Nothing that happened was your fault. This was Anton. Not you."

"Tell me we're safe."

"We're safe, baby. I wouldn't let anything happen to you."

****

Kasey's pussy tasted so damn good. Chip licked her clit, sliding his tongue back and forth before plunging down into her cunt. She tightened around him, and he loved that no other man had ever gotten a taste of her. She belonged completely to him, and he wouldn't let any other man take his place.

"That feels so good," she said, gasping as he plunged two fingers deep inside her.

His cock was so hard it hurt for him to move.

Working her pussy, he sucked her clit into his mouth using his teeth on the nub, which drew a scream from her. He loved the sounds she made as they echoed throughout the room. He'd never get tired of hearing her come.

They were the best sounds in the world, as far as he was concerned.

"Yes, yes, yes," she said.

Her orgasm began to build, and he worked her pussy until he threw her over the edge, and she went with a cry.

Licking up her cream, he kept her there, right at the peak, hurtling her into a second orgasm. He didn't want her to stop thinking about what they were doing for a single second.

Pressing a final kiss to her clit, he moved over her, holding Kasey in his arms.

She rolled over, her hand going to his stomach. Her cheeks were a shade of pink, and a hint of a smile was on her lips.

He'd imagined this moment so many times, in different ways.

"What about you?" she asked.

Chip took hold of her hand as she was about to cup his dick. "Tonight was about you. You taste amazing." He kissed her hand, and she pulled away, pushing him to the bed.

"I'm not a selfish person, Rufus Jones."

He groaned as she used his real name. "Can't you forget I told you that?"

"Nope. I like it." She moved to straddle his waist, and he cupped her ass, holding her still. Her pussy rested just above his dick. Her hands went to rest either side of his head. "What was I saying? Ah, yes, I'm not a selfish person, and you're not going to go without."

She leaned down, kissing his neck, sucking on the pulse.

He gasped as pleasure rushed through him. Sliding his hand up her back, he held her hand, tugging her down to claim her lips.

When he tried to push her so that she went to her back, she wouldn't let him, determined to stay in position.

"Nah, ah ah, I'm the one in charge right now." She eased up, moaning as he kneaded her ass cheeks.

All he wanted to do was lift her up, and slide her down on his dick, but he held off, loving the way she smiled at him, the wicked temptation on her lips as she sucked on the bottom one.

Releasing her ass, he held his hands above his head. "Okay. Do your worst. I am completely at your mercy."

"You're mine to do with as I please?"

"Yes. Whatever you want, just do it. Take what you want, baby."

"Now that is a tempting offer."

She placed her hands at his wrists, holding them either side of his head, giggling as he pretended to fight her.

"I've got you now," she said.

No, he had her, and he'd always have her. Nothing would change that.

She took his lips once again, and he'd never been one to enjoy kisses. He often found them overrated. When it came to Kasey though, he was starting to see the appeal. She broke the kiss first, and began to work her lips down, flicking his nipples with her tongue, and down even more, licking a path toward his dick.

When she moved between his thighs, he sat up to watch as she wrapped her fingers around the length. From the base up to the tip, she worked her hand over him. Pre-cum was already leaking out of the tip, so she used it to coat his length.

He was hard as a fucking rock.

She licked the tip, sucking off his cum before taking the entire head of his dick into her mouth.

Kasey moaned, the vibration going up the length of his cock at the same time she took him to the back of her throat, pulling off him as he did.

Keeping the head of his dick in her mouth, she

began to bob, and he reached down to move her hair out of the way so that he could get a good look at her sucking on his dick.

She glanced up at him, and he stroked her cheek.

"So pretty, baby. So pretty seeing that mouth of yours on my dick."

He hit the back of her throat once again, only this time, she didn't stop, swallowing more of him down, and he cursed, the pleasure sending another wave of pre-cum coating her throat.

She swallowed it down. Clenching his hands into fists, he tried to keep his composure, to not just spill his cum into her mouth, but it was next to impossible to do. Her mouth felt so good, and he'd imagined this for a long fucking time, even before he'd realized that he wanted Kasey as his own.

Kasey had become the woman he imagined. The woman he wanted.

The first time he'd seen her was all those years ago when Crazy had been at the hospital. It had only been a passing glance at the time, and he'd not known much about her. Over the past couple of years, he'd seen her on and off, but never known her name. Just knowing that he liked to look at her. At times he'd followed her to make sure she got home safely, being the caring fellow that he was.

At the funeral, Crazy had finally told him her name, and everything had clicked into place in his head.

"Fuck, baby, if you don't stop, I'm going to come. If you don't want my load in your mouth, pull up."

The pleasure was intense but Kasey didn't stop, and he groaned as she kept on sucking his cock.

Spilling his cum into her mouth, he felt her swallow him down, taking every single drop and not wasting any of it.

She licked his cock clean, and he stared down at her, stroking her cheek.

This was the woman he wanted to spend the rest of his life with.

****

There was always someone else who was the boss. He should have known, and should have done this long before he ever talked to Abelli, but this was supposed to be a family matter. Duke waited as he watched the car pulling into the lot. This was a very private meeting. Duke hadn't told anyone of what he was doing, but if everything went as planned tonight, he'd let his club know what he'd put in motion.

The Capo family were the ones he should have gone to. The Abellis held a great deal of power, but the one holding all the families together was none other than Alexander Capo.

"I want you to know this is absurd, and entirely embarrassing to be meeting at such a place," Alexander said.

"If I could have found a better place, I would have." Duke held out his hand. "It's a pleasure to meet you."

"I wouldn't say the same if it wasn't for the unpleasant business we need to discuss."

Duke wasn't a stupid man. He was aware that going after the Abelli line would come with severe consequences. No one took out a member of the mafia and lived all that much longer afterward. They were a close family, tightly-knit, and prided themselves on being a force to reckon with.

He'd been getting word that Abelli wasn't as well liked as he'd originally thought. Francis Abelli had to constantly clean up Anton's messes, and because of that, it had made him a weak link within.

"Francis Abelli. I want him dead, at my hands, at my club's hands," Duke said.

Alexander urged his guards to back down, and turned toward him. "I'm listening."

"I know if I take out Abelli, I'll be disrespecting you, which is why I've come to you. I'm aware of your embarrassment over what Anton caused."

The man before him cursed. "That man is a fucking pig. Getting your own daughter beaten and gang-raped, then to have it recorded for others to see." He spat on the ground. "The worst insult to our names. Abelli is supposed to reflect all of us, and he's caused nothing but grief."

"The Capo want him gone?" Duke asked.

Alexander took a long inhale on his cigar. "What do you want?"

"I'm killing Abelli no matter what. Now, you can see it as I'm doing you and your friends a favor, or you can see it as a slight against you. I don't want my club harmed."

"You're asking me for permission," Alexander said.

"I'm Prez of the Trojans MC. I don't ask for permission."

The man before him laughed. "I like you, Duke. You dealt with Anton in the way the Capo was going to do it. He couldn't have lived after what he did to his daughter. Francis kept protecting him. Now that we hear he's trying to hurt our good friends the Trojans MC, we're more than happy for you to deal with our problem, and we will look the other way."

Duke held out his hand, and Alexander took it. They both had a strong grip. Both of them were masters in their worlds, and neither of them was backing down.

"Do what needs to be done. I will alert the other

families, and once it's done, we will not hear from each other again," Alexander said.

"What? You don't want to be my new best friend?" Duke asked.

Alexander laughed. They pulled away, and Duke stayed in his spot as he watched the Capo family leave.

He had what he wanted, and now it was time to update the club.

Chapter Seven

One week later on Monday

"Duke called church for tonight," Brass said.

Chip moved out from the under the car he'd been looking over, and frowned. "What?"

"You heard me. He's called church, and wants everyone to be here."

"That's not totally unusual," Pie said.

Everything had returned to normal since Holly's Sunday dinner over a week ago. She'd spent more time around the club, and work had gone back to shift work. Chip worked four mornings a week in the mechanic shop in between other Trojan work and investments.

He looked at Brass, Pie, and Crazy. They all looked deep in thought.

"This is not normal. If you guys want to pretend it is, be my guest, but we all know something is going to kick off," Chip said.

"War with the Abelli mafia is guaranteed death," Crazy said. "Not to mention what it can do to the town."

"Duke's not after a war," Pie said.

"How can you be sure?" Brass asked.

"Duke got everything settled with Abelli after he took out Anton." Pie spoke up once again.

"I don't know. Tensions have been brewing for some time now, and I know he got Raoul to bring Diaz in."

Diaz's crew helped the Trojans out from time to time. He'd been friends with Raoul for as long as Chip could remember. Diaz had a way of getting information. His crew ruled the streets, and found that walls really did talk.

Chip stood up, cleaning off his wrench. "The way

I see it, we'll follow Duke no matter what. Francis screwed up when Anton got Russ and Sheila killed. The bargain we all struck was for them to live. That didn't happen. Two lives for one when Duke got Anton. He showed Francis respect by not taking out one of his other kids. He could have killed Maya, his granddaughter, or one of the daughters."

They all knew that Duke wasn't afraid to kill a woman. He'd done it before, and anyone who got in his way or hurt his woman had to face the consequences, and that was his wrath.

"Why don't we stop speculating like a bunch of pussies and get some work done? We'll find everything out at church and not a moment before," Chip said.

They all went to work on their cars or in the main office.

Chip was about to get back under his car when he saw Kasey park outside the shop.

He walked toward her as she skipped the last of the way, throwing herself into his arms.

"Be careful. I'll get you all dirty," he said.

"I don't care about a bit of grease. I'm normally covered in blood, crap, or vomit. This is a step up." She chuckled.

"This is a nice surprise." He rested his hands at the base of her back.

"I bought you lunch," she said, pulling out of his arms and reaching into her car.

He admired her ass, knowing later tonight he was going to have that nestled against his cock.

They hadn't had sex yet. Kasey wasn't ready, and he didn't mind waiting, especially as it gave them time to explore other things. He particularly loved the feel of her mouth on his dick. He also loved the taste of her pussy.

She lifted up, presenting him with a bag.

"Come on, we'll eat it in the office." Taking her hand, he nodded at the guys, who offered a hello to Kasey.

She said hello back. Chip tugged her into the office, slammed the door closed, and pressed her up against it.

Her arms went around his neck, pressing herself against him, and he groaned. Cupping her ass, he pulled her close, wanting nothing more than to fuck her right there and then.

He suddenly found a downfall with waiting for sex.

Moments like this, he craved it even more

Also, blue balls were overrated.

Someone cleared their throat, and releasing Kasey, he turned to find Pie sitting in the office. He'd not seen him when he entered, but he'd not been paying that much attention.

"You don't have to stop for me. That was getting me all worked up," Pie said.

Kasey groaned, wrapping her arms around his back, and resting her cheek against him.

"You've seen all you're going to see." Opening the door, he waited for Pie to leave.

Pie stopped beside Kasey. "Just out of curiosity, if I'd tried a little harder, would you have at least wanted me?"

Chip was ready to wipe the smirk off his face when he felt Kasey shake her head.

"No, I'm afraid not. I like you, Pie, but I think of you as a friend."

"Figures. I'm friend material." Pie winked at her, and closed the door. Chip shoved it the last bit, slamming it.

"You don't have to do that," she said, giggling.

"Did he really want to date me?"

"He was interested in you."

"He didn't try all that hard. It takes more than a bunch of flowers to get a woman's attention," she said.

"Oh yeah, what else does a guy need to do? Should I take notes?"

"Yes, lots and lots of notes." She hugged him close. "Let's see. You need to stop by a woman's house, and not flirt with her very sexy neighbor. Flowers are a must. So is dinner. Oh, and you have to have a very wicked tongue that makes a woman forget all of her prudish ways."

He took her lips once again. He couldn't resist those luscious lips, so sexy and hot.

"Are you taking notes?" she asked.

"That's what my head is. Lots of notes, and I'll be sure to show you exactly how good my tongue is."

He pressed her back up the wall, and she wrapped a leg around his waist, rubbing herself against him.

"We have to stop. I came to bring you lunch." She still held the lunch in her grip.

One final kiss and he stepped back, pulling out a chair for her to sit in.

"I could get used to this," he said.

He took the bag, opening it up to find a couple of sandwiches.

"I've got to go shopping, which is where I'm heading to next. I just wanted to stop by and see how you are."

"I'm doing good. I can't say the same about the car I'm working on. It's a piece of shit and falling apart." He took a bite of the cheese and pickle sandwich, enjoying it.

"Also, Holly invited me to a girls' night out," Kasey said.

"A girls' night?"

"Yeah. She said I could take Lindsey with me, and it'll be a lot of fun. Do you think I should go?" she asked.

He smiled. "I've got no problem with you hanging out with Holly and the old ladies. They'll keep you safe."

It was good that Holly was getting back into the swing of things.

"Speaking of plans. Do you mind sleeping over at the clubhouse Wednesday night? Duke's called church, and I've got to be there."

"Sure, I don't mind."

He finished the sandwich, wishing it would last longer.

Chip had watched each of the brothers fall for their woman. Little by little, they'd become smitten.

He wasn't going little by little. He'd fallen deeply, and it hadn't taken that long either.

Lunch ended all too soon, and he walked her back to her car.

Before she climbed in, she kissed him again, and he waited for her to leave before heading back to work.

"She's really taken with you," Pie said.

He stared at the brother, who looked a little envious. "You didn't want her."

"How do you figure that?"

"If you did, you wouldn't have given me a chance. You'd have been all over her just like you are every single club whore that steps through that door."

****

Wednesday night

Kasey stayed in the kitchen with Holly and the other old ladies. There were a couple of women she didn't recognize who kept a good distance from the old ladies. She sat beside Mary, who sipped at her water.

She was pregnant with her and Pike's second child. Zoe was also pregnant with Raoul's first child.

"Is it always like this?" she asked.

"Not always. This was an emergency meeting that Duke called. He rarely calls any of them," Holly said.

"And he rarely calls for Diaz's help," Zoe said. "I was with Raoul when he got the call to pick Diaz up and to meet him at the clubhouse."

"Is this about Francis?" Maya asked, speaking up.

Out of all of the women, Maya was the youngest of the bunch.

"I don't know," Holly said.

"You can't keep everyone in the dark. If you know something, you've got to tell," Maya said.

"I don't know anything. Honestly, I don't know."

Kasey didn't have a clue what was going on, so she sipped her drink and tried to think of other things. The women all looked somber. Maria, Daisy's woman, was pale, as was Beth, Knuckles's old lady.

So many names, and she couldn't remember them all, or all of their history.

"How are things going with you and Chip?" Leanna asked, leaning in close.

All of the kids were asleep in their rooms in the clubhouse. Chip had taken her for a tour around the large building. There was a boys' nursery and girls' nursery, where all the kids slept when they stayed at the clubhouse.

She also realized that when the kids were in residence, the clubhouse was very tame. Once the kids were gone, everyone came out to play.

"Really good. My neighbor adores him."

"I like Lindsey," Maria said. "She doesn't have a

filter, does she?"

Kasey laughed. "No. I've known her for some time now, and whatever she is thinking or feeling, she'll just spill it out. I like that about her."

"It's refreshing," Holly said, speaking up. "It's nice to know she's not trying to steal your man either."

Holly's gaze was on the girl that had been coming out of the same room as Pie.

Kasey glanced over at the woman, and saw she sat on her own. None of the other women sat with her.

"Why don't they sit closer to us?" she asked Leanna.

Leanna looked at the women. "They're sweet-butts or club whores. Whichever you want to call them. They … entertain the men."

"They fuck any and whichever member will have them. They don't get to pick and choose," Holly said. "Some of them also don't care if one or more of the guys are taken." Holly forced a smile to her lips. "A word of warning, some men struggle to stay faithful."

"Duke's not like that, and you know it."

"My dad wasn't faithful to my mother. He cheated on her. Our men haven't cheated," Holly said. "It can happen, though."

Kasey couldn't help but look at the other women and wonder if one or more of them had slept with Chip. If he'd fucked them in the bed that they had messed around in.

She was thirty, not old by any means, but to some, that was still too old. The women wore next to nothing. Shirts that outlined their braless state. Perky breasts, with their nipples pressing against the fabric. The shirts ended just under the breasts, revealing smooth stomachs. A couple of the women were fuller, curvier, and younger.

Suddenly hit with a wave of insecurity, Kasey wondered if it would be wrong to have a glass of brandy, or something stronger.

"Okay, you totally sucked all the fun out of the room," Zoe said. "It's not just club life. It's every kind of man *and* woman that can cheat. You can cheat just as much as Duke. We're not all perfect, and pretending we are is wrong."

"Do you know if…" Kasey stopped, biting her lip.

"You want to know if Chip has fucked any of those women?" Zoe asked.

She nodded, hating that she wanted to know.

"You'll have to ask him," Leanna said, speaking up once again.

Kasey had a feeling she really wasn't going to like the answer.

****

Duke, Pike, and Raoul were already in church when he arrived. Chip shook his head, waiting as brother after brother entered the church.

The last to arrive was Pie, who took a seat in the back.

The door closed, their cell phones taken, and silence filled the air. No one made a sound or a move.

Chip looked at Duke, waiting.

"I'm sure you're all curious as to why I called this meeting," Duke said. "I'm aware you all know that Diaz was here the other day. It has been brought to my attention that Abelli men have been in Vale Valley. They've been asking … questions. About the club. About my wife. About our families."

Chip didn't like that, and from the look on the brothers' faces, none of them were impressed.

"Tensions have been running high for some time

now. Some of you may or may not have agreed with me taking out Anton Abelli." He stopped.

"No, you had every single right to do that," Landon said.

Everyone agreed.

"He took Russ," Chip said. "And Sheila. You make a bargain, even with the devil, you expect to keep it. He had what was coming to him."

"I cannot allow this to stand. Vale Valley is Trojan land. This is our town, and I swear to you all, to the patch, and to my club, I will not see any Trojan under Abelli's thumb." The rage inside Duke was clear to see. He was shaking with it. "I vowed to lead you guys. To do everything in my power to protect the club. The moment you put your life with that of the mafia, you're no longer a club. You're dogs for them to call. I won't do that. This is *our* club. Our home. I'm going to send a message to Abelli in person. I've called a meeting with him for tomorrow. I'm going to see him. I have a package for him, about what we do to men who sneak around our town, asking questions."

Chip nodded.

"Taking out Abelli is not the only problem. I know he's one of many families within the mafia, so I arranged a meeting with its head, Alexander Capo. Since Francis kept protecting his son against the consequences of what he'd done, Capo wants Abelli gone. They will not cause us a problem once it's done. I know some of you don't want to go to war. They don't want to have the risk to their families and the club. Fine, get the fuck out. I mean it. We can vote on it. If I've not got a brother in this club willing to risk his life to protect my back and my family's back, then get out. We all made a vow when we took our patch. Your family is my family. I will risk my life for yours, and you will for mine. You don't want to do that, I don't want you in my club. You think you can do a better job at this, then come and take it, I fucking dare you to. Don't tell me how to protect this club. Don't stab me in the back. Come to me like a damn man, and tell me it straight."

Chip looked around the table, wondering if anyone was going to step up or leave.

Crazy sighed. "You know what, I think we've gotten too damn lazy. I'm done with the Abelli bullshit. Every time I see Holly, I see Maya, fuck, I see this damn clubhouse that Russ slaved away to build. He made this fucking club what it is, and that fucker's son took him from us. Nah, no, I don't give a shit anymore. That fucker wants a war. He wants to take on the Trojans. Bring it. I'm not someone's dog, and I sure as shit don't serve any mafia prick."

Everyone in the room cheered.

Before Russ's death, the club had been smoothly going about its business, doing the drug and gun runs that Ned Walker sent their way. They'd stayed in their own business. Then the Abelli truth had come out. The club had stumbled a little, pulling back to protect its own. With Russ's death, they'd been in shock, in mourning, each of them dealing with their grief in their own way.

If Abelli had left them alone, everything would have been fine. There wouldn't have been any danger. He hadn't walked away.

Invading their town, even if it was only one person, that was a sign of disrespect.

Now, he'd woken up a rage within the club. One of their men was down. The Trojans didn't take the death of one of their own easily.

They fought.

They killed.

They got vengeance.

It was time for the Trojans to take theirs, and Abelli better watch out, because once they started, only when the Trojans were ready, would they stop.

Chapter Eight

Kasey waited in the kitchen, and when church ended, she noticed all the somber expressions on the women around the table as one by one, their men came. The single men stayed in the main part of the clubhouse.

Chip stood in front of her, and she offered him a smile, which he returned but without much enthusiasm.

Something had gone bad.

"Can we go to my room?" he asked.

She took his hand, not arguing as he followed her upstairs.

"Everyone seemed tense going into the room, but they all look even worse coming out of it," she said.

He closed his bedroom door, and once again, she sat down at the end of his bed, waiting. Biting her lip, she was sure he was going to dump her. She didn't know why it felt like that, only that it did.

"Do you want me to leave?" she asked.

"No, of course not. Why would you think for even a second I'd want you to leave?"

"You're going to dump me, right? Isn't that why we're up here?" she asked.

He took her hand, pulling her to her feet and slamming his lips down on hers. All she wanted to do was hold him back, but she stopped herself, keeping her hands by her sides.

As the kiss progressed, she couldn't help but touch him.

Chip set a blaze within her, and made it next to impossible for her to think clearly with him so close.

"I'm not going to dump you. I should slap your ass for even thinking such stupid things."

She chuckled, opening her eyes, which had closed

during their kiss. "If you don't want to dump me, what's wrong?"

He stroked her cheek, like he'd done so many times before, and she saw the struggle inside him.

"You're my woman, right?" He looked her in the eye. "I'm not joking around. You're my old lady in everything."

"Like Holly?" she asked.

"Yes. You have my back, and that of the club. You don't rat on us no matter what you hear or what you know." He placed a hand at her heart. "Your loyalty is to the club and the people inside."

"Yes," she said. There was no way in hell that she'd ever allow any harm to come to the club or the people that served it. Over the years she'd come to see that the Trojans took care of each other.

"Agreeing to be my old lady, it's being my wife, Kasey."

"Are you asking me to marry you?"

"Yes, I am."

She gasped and looked at him. So many questions rushed through her head.

Did he love her?

Did he want to get married for real?

Did she love him?

What did he want from her?

"This isn't a church wedding, baby. Asking you to be my old lady is like marriage in the eyes of the club."

"Oh." She frowned. "You had me going for a second there."

He tilted her head back, staring into her eyes. "Then let me make it clear for you, Kasey. I love you. I've been in love with you for a considerable amount of time. I didn't act on it. For a long time, I didn't even know your name." His gaze moved down to her lips, and then back up. "When you're ready, I will ask you to marry me, but I don't expect you to fall for me in a couple of weeks. I know I'm not that good."

She chuckled.

"Something's about to happen at the club. Something big, and it's going to take me out of town for a couple of days."

"By something big, do you mean dangerous?"

"Yes."

Fear and panic gripped her. Nothing could happen to him.

"Don't go, please," she said, holding onto his arms, needing him to know that she couldn't stand it if something was to happen to him.

Just the thought of never being able to see him again...

She shook her head.

No!

She wouldn't think like that.

She couldn't.

Chip, Rufus Jones, was part of her life now.

"I've got to. I'm not a coward."

"They'll know that, Chip. They'll know that you're not a coward."

He held her close, and she rested her head against his chest, not wanting to let him go. She couldn't. What would she do if he didn't make it? Dangerous meant he could be hurt or worse, killed.

She wasn't some naïve person. Kasey was all too aware that the club was real, not some fake imitation. They did what they had to in order to survive.

The deaths of Russ and Sheila had confirmed that they were not a completely innocent club. She didn't care, though.

Crazy, Leanna, Holly, Mary, and now Chip had all become part of her world. They were her friends, and Chip was the man she … cared about? No, she didn't just care about him.

Her feelings for him were so much stronger than that.

"You can ask me anything in the world. I'll do my best to give you every single thing that your heart desires, but don't ever ask me to leave my club in the lurch."

"I'm not." She cupped the back of his head, bringing it down, so that she could kiss his lips.

The moment his lips were on hers, everything seemed clearer, right, and perfect. Kissing him back with a passion, she moaned, needing him so damn much.

Heat flooded her pussy, and her nipples tightened to unbearable points.

"I can't stand the thought of anything bad happening to you, but I'd never, ever, ask you to turn your back on the club." She broke from the kiss and ran her hands beneath his leather cut.

Sliding her hands up, she pushed the leather from his arms, hearing it fall to the floor. Tugging her own shirt off, she went to his, pulling it off as he unsnapped her bra. She attacked his jeans at the same time as he took hers away, and once they were completely naked, she sank to the floor before him.

Wrapping her fingers around his rock-hard cock, she licked the tip, which already had a copious amount of pre-cum spilling out of the tip. The moment she covered the head with her mouth, he released a little hiss, and she chuckled, taking more of him into her mouth. She loved the taste of him as he slid down her throat.

Pulling off his cock, she worked the length, watching as pre-cum leaked out of the slit at the head of him.

It was so sexy.

Staring up at him, she saw the desire, the need shining right back at her.

"Do you have any idea how much I want to fuck you right now?"

She licked her lips and nodded. "Then do it."

"What?"

"I want you to fuck me, Chip." She licked his cock. "Do what you want with me."

She'd been waiting for the right time, and then she finally realized that no time would ever be the right time. Her nerves would never just disappear. She'd always be waiting.

Chip made her feel so much. He made her comfortable to be herself, and he always made her laugh. When they weren't together, she always thought about him, hoping he was having a good time.

He dominated her thoughts.

Lindsey had told her that someone who dominated thoughts the way she described, it had to be love.

Again, she didn't want to put a label on anything for fear of it ruining whatever they'd begun. She knew he loved her, and she loved him, but … fear was a horrible thing, and right now, she was afraid to lose him. She'd been along for so long, so it was almost too much to hope that someone might want her as much as she wanted him.

He took her hand once again, lifting her to her feet. He sank his fingers into her hair, slamming his lips down on hers, making her melt against him.

"Do you have any idea at all what you do to me? What I want to do to you?" he asked.

"I'm hoping it's something good," she said, teasing him.

"More than good. I can promise you, babe, you won't be thinking of anyone else by the time I've finished fucking you."

"Chip, I don't think of anyone else. There's no one else in my life that I'll ever want or need. It's only you. It will only ever be—"

He silenced her with his lips, and she moaned, wrapping her arms around him at the same time, he moved her toward the bed.

She dropped down on it, breaking the kiss and intending to move up the bed, but he stopped her by wrapping his hand around her leg. He knelt down on the floor, and she followed his instructions putting both feet at the edge, and placing her ass close to the edge of the bed.

The position exposed her pussy, and Chip stared down at her.

She'd never been one to remove all of her pubic hair, as she didn't like the feel of it when it grew back, so she kept it neatly trimmed.

"Do you have any idea how pretty this pussy looks?"

"No," she said, smiling.

"It's going to look even better when you take my cock."

Biting her lip, she nodded.

"You do that a lot, you know," he said.

"What?"

"Biting your lip. Do I make you nervous?"

"No. You don't make me nervous."

"What do I make you, baby?" he asked.

"You make me burn, and I can't seem to help it. It's bite my lip or moan."

"Then moan. I want to hear those sounds coming from you."

CRAVE

****

Chip ran his fingers across her pussy, watching as her head moved back just a little, and a little gasp escaped her followed by the sexiest moan he'd ever heard. Sliding two fingers between her slit, he circled her swollen nub, marveling at how wet she was.

He'd licked and played with this pussy many times over the past few days, and he loved how slick and ready she was. She'd admitted to him just the other day that she'd only had sex with one person, and since then, all she'd done was pleasure herself.

Since then, he'd been determined to drive her crazy with need, to watch as each time he touched her, she fell apart, needing him even more.

The club was heading into serious danger. He got that, understood it, and there was a small smidgen of a chance that this wouldn't blow up in all of their faces. Of course, there was also a large chance he'd be dead by the end of the week.

With that thought in mind, he filled her cunt with his two fingers watching as her hole stretched around him. Pulling out, he saw her cream soaking his digits, and he plunged them inside again.

Removing his fingers from her pussy, he replaced them with his tongue, sliding inside her, fucking her, tasting her before licking up to her clit and circling the hard bud. Over, around, and flicking across, he teased her clit, sucking it deep into his mouth.

She touched his head, and he grabbed her hands in both of his, locking them against the bed, holding her still as he ravished her tasty cunt.

"Oh, fuck, that feels ... don't stop, Chip. Please, don't stop."

He licked her pussy, sliding down to her cunt, then up to her clit and down again, each time driving her closer to orgasm. Her pussy tightened for him to see.

When he no longer could stand to keep her waiting anymore, he focused on her pretty clit, bringing her to an orgasm that had her screaming for him not to stop.

It wasn't long before she pleaded for him to stop, but he wasn't a man who liked odd numbers. He wanted to even things out, so he hurtled her into a second orgasm, relishing her cries as her pussy completely relented to his tongue.

He didn't give her any time to come down from that second orgasm. Pushing her to the bed, he grabbed a condom, tearing into the latex and rolling it down his cock. Moving between her thighs, he rubbed his cock between her slick folds, wishing nothing was between them, but knowing that would come all too soon, and he was a very patient man.

With the head of his cock at her entrance, he slowly began to fill her, shocked by how tight she actually was.

Holding his cock until the first couple of inches were inside her, he slammed the last few to the hilt, taking hold of her hands and keeping them captive above her head, locking them there.

"I've got you now, baby. You're completely at my mercy," he said.

She wriggled her pussy onto his cock and smiled. "I don't mind being at your mercy. You can have and do whatever you want with me. You're my master."

His cock pulsed at her words, and he pulled out only to slam back inside, going deeper than before.

They both moaned, and he couldn't resist. Pulling out of her tight heat, he slammed inside her, going deeper with every single thrust.

"Oh, my God," she said, screaming.

"Not God, me. I'm the one fucking you, baby." He pounded inside her so hard that the headboard slammed against the wall.

Chip didn't care. All he wanted to do was fuck her, take her so hard, and have her screaming and begging for more.

He didn't want it to stop, so before he found that peak, Chip pulled out of her and held himself poised between her thighs.

"What is it?" she asked, panting.

"I'm not ready to finish, not yet. I don't want this to end just yet." His cock was still rock-hard, but he was back in control now. He slid his cock through her pussy, coating his condom-covered dick in her cream.

With each bump against her clit, she released a little moan, going deeper with each touch on her pussy.

"Please, Chip, fuck me," she said.

"I will fuck you."

With his grip on her hips, he moved her so that she was on her knees, her glorious ass presented to him. He ran his fingers over her cheeks, spreading them open to look at her anus and cunt.

Her cunt was slick, and he slid two fingers within her tightness.

"I'm going to have to fuck you a lot more so that you get used to me."

"I've got no problem with that," she said, glancing over her shoulder at him. The wicked smile on her lips drew another from him.

"You're a temptress, you know that, right?"

"I know that I want you, and you've stopped fucking me."

He then grabbed his cock and fucked her hard, slamming deep as he took hold of her hips, and used them to pound inside her soaked cunt.

They both moaned, and he fucked her harder, watching as his dick filled her pussy. The lips wrapped around his length, and the tight heat was like a vise around his dick.

Slamming his length hard and deep, he paused all the way inside her. The pleasure was out of this world, and he'd never been this close to coming so quickly before.

He didn't want to stop.

Suddenly, Kasey pulled off his cock, and turned toward him so that she was kneeling on the bed, matching him.

She wrapped her arms around his neck, kissing his lips, trailing them to his ear. "It doesn't have to be just one time," she said. "I don't mind if I spend the entire night fucking you, Chip. You don't have to make this last."

He had her on her back with his cock deep inside her within a matter of seconds.

He slammed into her over and over, feeling the pleasure tightening his balls, wanting to go deeper still. Holding her hands, he pressed them against her head, liking how it put her at his mercy, keeping her under his control so that he could do whatever he liked with her body, and he intended to do a lot to her, to fuck her until she could no longer think straight and then some.

"Please, don't stop," she said.

Her pussy tightened as he fucked her harder than before. He glanced down, watching as his cock filled her, and the pleasure was something he couldn't control.

After several thrusts, he came, filling the condom with his cum.

He wrapped his arms around her, keeping his dick inside her, not wanting to leave her body, or for this to end.

Staring into her eyes, he gripped her ass, kneading the flesh.

"That was amazing," she said.

"It wasn't my best performance."

"Are you kidding right now?"

"I've been wanting to be inside you for a long time, Kasey. I rushed it. I couldn't help it. You drive me wild."

She chuckled. "I like that. I like that I drive you wild, and you can't help it when you're fucking me."

"Don't worry. I reckon in a couple of years, I'll last ten minutes longer," he said, teasing.

She stroked his cheek, and the smile on her lips did something inside him. The beauty of her, the kindness, everything about her just filled him with so much love and joy.

"There's nowhere else I'd rather be than with you right now," he said.

"Me neither. I like being with you, Chip. So much at times that it scares me."

"Don't let it."

"I don't want to turn into one of those women who can't seem to function without her man around, you know? Always checking her phone, and nagging about him."

"I'll never cheat on you if that's what you're worried about," he said.

"It's not. Well, Holly said something about men always cheating, but then Zoe said that *any* man not just a biker cheats, and right now I'm rambling. The after sex thing is new to me."

"As much as it kills me to say this, what normally happens after sex for you?" he asked. He didn't like the thought of another man touching her.

She belonged to him.

"Do you really want me to talk about this right now?"

"Nope, I really don't, but I also don't want us to keep any secrets from each other."

"Okay, erm, let's see. After sex, talking about it with my current boyfriend, about my past boyfriends. He'd climb off, and I'd go to the bathroom, and I tended to have a shower. He never stayed the night, and I always saw him to the door like the nice, polite girl that I am."

"Sounds so prim and proper," he said.

"I'm very prim and proper."

"Are you wanting to run to the shower right now?"

She shook her head. "Nah, I don't even want to leave this bed." She placed her hand over his chest. "There's something I told Pie that I never told you before, and I don't like that he knows, and you don't."

"What is it?"

"It's about what happened after my brother died."

He listened as she told him about the darkness, about how close she came to losing it, and only the memory of her brother pulled her out of the pain she'd been feeling.

"That's what Pie knows?"

"Yes. We talked about it, and I didn't want you to think for a second he was more important—"

He silenced her with a kiss.

"No, I don't even think that, not even for a second. I will do everything in my power to make you happy."

The smile on her face filled with sadness. "Then please don't be a hero with whatever danger you're going to face. I don't think I could bear anything happening to you."

He pulled her close and held her tightly.

No matter what, Chip knew he couldn't die. Something told him that if he did, it could push Kasey over the edge, and he wouldn't let that happen.

Chapter Nine

With all of his men gone, Duke stood and went to the window overlooking the main back yard of the clubhouse. He'd installed a play area for the kids some time ago, and often he'd stand at this window and watch them play.

There had been many times he'd watched Holly as well, keeping an eye on her, hoping she'd take advantage of the other old ladies watching their babies so that she'd sneak into his office, and they'd get some alone time.

"You don't think this is a bit extreme? Going to Capo, arranging this?" Pike asked, pointing at the cool box where he'd placed his present for Abelli.

Diaz, Raoul, and Pike had captured the man who'd been asking a lot of questions he should. Duke had simply removed that head from his body. The moment he'd gone to the basement and begun talking with Abelli's man, hearing that Francis wanted to know everything that was going on in the Trojans MC,

Duke had lost it.

Between nearly losing his wife to whatever fear that had gripped her, the loss of Russ and Sheila, the pain he felt at the core within his club, he'd snapped.

The little messenger had paid the price with his life.

"The Capo wants them gone, Pike. I heard a story many years ago of someone who was in Abelli territory. He was asking a lot of questions, and so Francis Abelli did no more than take the man, torture him until he was unrecognizable, and then made an example of him by displaying his head on a pike within one of his warehouses. He'd done it to send a message out to anyone that would dare talk about him with anyone else." Duke looked at Pike. This was his right-hand man. The man he trusted to have his back.

Their wives were the best of friends, and he knew without a doubt that if anything happened to him, Pike would take care of his woman and kids, no questions asked.

"Sounds … crazy."

Duke nodded. "Abelli sent a messenger into my town and thought he could get away with it. I told him to leave us alone. I made it clear that under any circumstances he shouldn't make an enemy out of me." He'd kept Anton alive, and when Francis had come into the room, he'd made it clear that he would make Abelli's life a misery. He'd threatened to turn all evidence he had on Francis Abelli over to the police, to let them deal with him.

Francis had decided to leave, and promised not to return.

That hadn't lasted long. Between the flowers sent to his woman, and the guy walking his streets, whatever niceties that Duke had intended had long gone.

Maybe he was making a big deal over nothing. His club wouldn't stand down, nor would it give in to monsters like Abelli.

He wasn't a rat.

There's no way he'd hand anything over to the cops. Duke dealt with his problems himself, and the Trojans didn't walk away from a threat.

"I won't let him destroy this club."

"If this turns to shit, our entire club will be gone," Pike said. He didn't say it as a warning, merely a statement.

"You don't have to come. None of the club has to."

"You're insane, right? You're our Prez. If you think for a second that anyone would let you leave this on your own, you're even crazier than I thought. The club will be at your back, like always. Nothing is going to change that."

Pike held out his hand, and Duke took it.

"Brothers for life. I promised to serve you, Duke, and I don't see a problem with sending a message to Abelli."

****

Mary stared down at Starlight, who was already fast asleep. It had been a long day, and she tucked her hair behind her ears to look at her daughter. Glancing around the room, she saw all of the kids were asleep.

Movement toward the door had her turning to see Pike, her husband, there. The somber look on his face had her going to him. He took her hand and she closed the door.

"What's wrong?" she asked.

He didn't speak, waiting until they got to their own room.

Pike took a seat on the bed and pulled her between his thighs. He pressed kisses to her already swelling stomach, and she knew something bad was going to happen.

"What's going on, Pike?"

"I'm heading out tomorrow with Duke."

"Is this about the Abelli problem?" she asked.

She knew Abelli had been causing a few troubles. Holly had finally told her everything, and she knew the club wouldn't let Abelli's interference stand.

"Yes. We're going to do what is right for the club."

"It's dangerous?"

He didn't say anything, pressing kisses to her

stomach, and she closed her eyes, feeling her eyes begin to fill. This was their perfect little family, and she didn't want to lose that.

"There's money in the safe at home. You know the combination, and I've also put enough aside for you so that you'll never have to worry."

"Pike?"

"Go to Mac. He'll get you out of town, and take Holly with you."

"No, Pike. Don't."

"I will always put something in place to take care of you. I have no intention of dying tomorrow, but if I do, know that I love you more than anything else in the world."

She shook her head. "Not this."

He pulled her into his arms and took her down to the bed, kissing her lips.

Mary loved this man more than she loved anyone else in the world. She couldn't imagine being without him. Mac had been a problem between them in the past, and she couldn't imagine Pike trusting him.

"Do you really think it could end like that?" she asked.

"I don't know how it will end. It all depends on how stubborn Duke and Abelli are."

She took a deep breath. "I ... please, don't do anything that will get you killed."

"I won't, babe."

They both knew it was a lie. Pike would stay to defend Duke. He'd stay to protect him to the bitter end.

Holding him tightly, Mary prayed that nothing bad would happen. Not when everything had been going so well between them. They didn't have the easiest of relationships, as it had been fraught at times. It didn't stop her from loving him, though. She'd never stop loving him, not ever.

****

Zoe didn't need to be told that shit was going down. Raoul never kept a single secret from her, and as she stood outside, he moved up behind her, wrapping his arms around her waist.

She stared up at the moon, marveling at its beauty filling the sky.

"You know, on the opposite side of the world, it's daytime, and to think that they're living the next day while we're finishing this one, it's kind of surreal, don't you think?"

"It certainly puts a great deal into perspective."

"The world is bigger than just one of us. It's made of many people, many things, and it means you don't have to follow the rules. You don't have to ... do something that could get you killed."

She turned in his arms, seeing the pain in his eyes and wishing it was different.

"I can't do what you need me to do, Zoe. My club needs me."

Grabbing his hand, she placed it on her stomach. "I need you. We need you."

"Zoe?"

"I know. I know. No matter what I say. No matter what I ask. You're going to go, but please know that I love you. I love you and this club, and even though it kills me to know you'll be going out there, and possibly getting killed, I will still love you."

He gripped the back of her head and kissed her.

Zoe held onto his leather jacket, unable to deal with the pain that was currently filling her chest. She had fallen for Raoul, and over the years that love had gotten deeper. The thought of anything happening to him created a pain unlike anything she'd ever felt or known.

She didn't want to think about it, and refused to believe that anything could happen to him.

"I love you, Zoe. You and our child." He placed a hand on her stomach, and she rested her head against his chest, not wanting to let him go.

****

Leanna was already crying when Crazy carried her to their room. They didn't spend that much time at the clubhouse anymore, but the time they did was often filled with lots of dirty sex where she didn't have to worry about making any noise.

"I know, baby. I know." They lay on the bed, wrapped around each other.

She didn't tell him that he didn't have to go as she already knew that he would. Nothing would stop him from going, nothing.

"I know without a shadow of a doubt that you would take care of our children. That you'll love them, and give them a life no matter what happens." He kissed her lips, and like the first time, she fell for him a little bit more.

She'd been taking care of Strawberry when his wife at the time would dump her because she really hadn't wanted a kid.

Leanna loved Strawberry as if she were her own. She'd taken care of her so much that Strawberry even called her "mother," and if Suz—Crazy's ex—came to pick her up, she'd scream and cry.

It didn't matter if she told him not to go. In the time she spent at the club, she knew the brothers were bound together, and she'd never forgive herself if for even a second, something happened and Crazy hadn't been there because of her.

"I love you," she said.

He kissed her at the same time he began to

remove her clothing. She didn't fight him. There were no words. She craved him just as he much as he did her.

****

"Please, don't say anything. Don't tell me that I'll be happy, and that you've gotten everything ready so that I'll live a happy life. Me and Tanya," Maria said, looking at Daisy.

He didn't say anything.

Instead, he walked up to her, pulling Maria into his arms, and holding her tightly to him. He loved this woman more than anything else. She'd become part of him, showing her every single day that until he had her in his life, he'd only been partly living, never really grasping what he'd been missing out on.

"Everything is going to be okay."

"You can't guarantee that."

"I trust Duke. He's never steered us wrong, and he's not going to do it now." He cupped her face, forcing her to gaze into his eyes. "I'm not a stupid man, baby. I wouldn't put you or our little girl in danger."

She took a deep breath. "You're going to pick a fight. You told me that Abelli is not a man to mess with."

"Neither is our club, and I'm not going to stand back while he does what he does." He kissed her lips. Whatever happened, Daisy believed deep in his heart that taking the fight to Abelli was the right thing to do.

Sitting back and doing nothing, letting this slight go unpunished would only open them up to further attack.

He wouldn't bring that kind of pain to his town, to his family.

****

"I've been thinking what to say to you," Beth said. "I can't ... I'm ... in a pretty bad place right about now."

Knuckles stared at his blonde, beautiful woman. She owned his heart, his soul, was his very reason for breathing. He'd gone head to head with Daisy to prove his love for this woman. She'd gotten under his skin, inside his heart, and there wasn't a person in the world that could ever do that to him.

He imagined each of the brothers were doing this right now. The old ladies had been together in the kitchen, waiting, expecting the outcome.

Beth knew even before he came to her.

Pressing his head against hers, he didn't say anything.

There was nothing to say.

He wouldn't let Duke ride out to Abelli alone. The club was strong together, and with that, they were all going to fight for their club.

****

"Are you wishing you married someone else right now?" Brass asked.

His naked wife pressed against his side.

"No, I don't wish that for a second," Eliza said. "I know you've got to do what you've got to do."

He kissed the top of her head.

Her hand rested on his stomach.

"Duke's a good man," he said.

"I know. I'm not going to beg or ask you to stay at home. I know you can't do that, but please be safe." She looked up at him. "I love you. Your greasy bike, and dirty sex. I couldn't be without you, and I don't ever want to think about a life without you either."

"You've got no chance of that ever happening." He took a deep breath. "What will probably happen is Duke will pull his dick out, Abelli will do the same, and we'll all be in a room with a ruler, measuring how big our dicks are. We'll win," he said. She laughed. "You know it."

"You're so bad. We shouldn't be laughing about this."

"I don't want my night here to be filled with you worrying," he said, stroking his thumb down her arm.

"You're not worried?"

He thought about it, and shook his head. "No."

"Why not?"

"What will be will be, and nothing is going to change that." He kissed her lips. "Just think of a roomful of men measuring their cocks."

"You should totally send a selfie of that, and send it to me."

Brass knew she played along with him, and he didn't blame her at all. The threat they faced was real.

****

"Dad," Matthew said, staring at his father's back. For the first time in his life, he saw Duke looking so fucking cold.

"What's the matter, son?"

"I want to come tomorrow."

"No. You're not coming." Duke moved toward him, putting his hands on his shoulders. "I need you home."

"Tell me how real this threat is and be honest. Don't lie." Matthew knew the club didn't always handle legal shit. He wasn't a fool, and knew that Abelli wasn't something to be happy about.

In the past month his father had aged some. The darkness in his eyes was clear to see, and that of Holly's.

"It can go two ways. Abelli listens to me, understands that I mean business, and we leave. He doesn't come near Vale Valley, and I don't hunt every single business he has, and cost him a fortune."

"Or?"

"Or we'll be digging some graves."

Matthew gritted his teeth. "I don't want anything bad to happen."

"Do you love Luna?" Duke asked.

"What?"

"I'm not an idiot, son. You've made it so she can go away to college, and I saw the way you looked at her. You nearly knocked her up."

"That's all in the past."

"Life has taught me one thing, Matthew, don't let the girl of your dreams get away. This life, it'll swallow you up, and spit you back out when it's done. What makes life bearable is having a woman that you love, and a family at your back. Remember that."

Duke tapped his face with a smile, and turned to leave.

"Love you, Dad."

"Love you, too, son."

Watching his father go, Matthew pulled out his cell phone and stared down at Luna's number.

He'd been tempted to call and to text her for some time, but he'd held off, always finding a reason not to do it.

Taking his father's advice, he sent a text.

Matthew: I hope college is treating you well. Kind of dull around here at mo. Got any gossip to keep me alive?

****

Holly waited on the stairs, stopping Duke's climb. She'd heard what he said to Matthew, and his words touched her heart.

She stared at the man she'd tried not to fall in love with, but it had been inevitable. There was no way she couldn't love him. Duke moved toward her, captured her lips, and with ease, he lifted her up, carrying her through to their bedroom.

Words were not needed. They'd been together long enough to know that they loved each other.

****

Maya stood in the doorway of Landon's room. She knew what was going to happen, and she'd come to see Landon as a brother.

"Are you okay?" she asked.

He looked up.

The entire club was on a point of no return.

Her grandfather sending that man started a turning point. She hoped nothing happened to the men in the club.

"Yeah, I'm good. You know we're heading out tomorrow?"

She nodded.

"You got any words of advice?"

Maya stared at the floor. "His strongest men won't be behind him. They'll be the men closest to you, and they'll have one hand on their gun at all times. They're fast. Take them out, and you might surprise him."

Landon chuckled. "I don't see Francis Abelli only having two strong men."

She shrugged. "It's what I remember my father telling me. You're like a brother to me, Landon. Please don't get killed."

"I don't plan to."

Chapter Ten

Kasey woke the following morning with a smile on her face as she stared at Chip. He was wide awake. Slowly, she saw that not only was Chip awake, but he was also dressed.

The memory of the night before came rushing back to her.

"Today?"

"Yes. Everyone is getting ready downstairs." He held a mug up. "I brought you coffee."

She sat up in the bed, lifting the blanket as she did. The pleasure of the night before ebbed away as she looked at Chip. His hair was slicked back from running his fingers through it so often.

"How long have you been awake?"

"About an hour. I didn't want to waste a moment of my time with you." She took the cup from him, taking a sip of the coffee. It tasted good with a hint of vanilla.

"This is good."

"Duke loves a good cup of coffee. There's always some weird syrup shit to put in it."

She chuckled.

"How long do we have?" she asked.

He started to laugh. "Come on. Don't do that. This isn't bad or anything. I'm not never coming home."

"But the risk is still there, right? You may not make it home."

"I'll come home." He kissed her lips. "Now drink that coffee, and stop worrying. You've got work today?"

"Yes."

"I'll keep in constant contact with you. That way you won't be worrying about the little things."

"I don't think I'll ever stop worrying about you."

He smiled. "I'm not going to complain like that."

She smiled.

"So, when I get back, will you still be my old lady?" he asked.

Kasey smiled. "Nothing has changed since last night, and I have to say with how good last night was, I don't see anything changing any time soon."

"Good, because, there's kind of a ... ceremony that we need to complete. It's nothing bad, but we'll talk about it more."

"Will I have to give my blood or take a special oath?"

"Nope. You'll just have to declare your loyalty to me and to the club."

She nodded, staring at the cup. "Chip, I want to say something to you, but I don't want you to give it much thought not until you come home."

"I'm listening."

Licking her dry lips, she took a deep breath, and stared into his eyes. "Are you ready?"

He laughed. "Yes. I'm ready."

"I love you."

Silence met her words, and she watched the shock cross his face, and thought it was so cute to have taken him by surprise.

He went to say something, but she stopped him with a finger across his lips. "No, you don't get to say anything. That was what I wanted to say to you. I don't expect you to say anything, but I want you to know we should talk about that when you get back."

She wasn't even for a second going to think that he wasn't coming back. She couldn't.

Moving a finger from his lips, she smiled at him.

Finishing off her coffee, she climbed out of bed and quickly changed into her clothes, running a brush through her hair.

Taking his hand, they walked downstairs, and she noticed nearly all of the men were outside waiting.

She stood by Chip's side as they all turned toward Duke, who was the last to come out of the house.

"You don't all have to come with me," Duke said.

"There's no chance you're getting away with looking like the biggest badass out there," Pie said.

"We've all got reputations to protect." This came from Floss.

"I want to kick some ass," Landon said.

"You're not alone," Pike said. "The club stands behind you."

"For Russ," Raoul said.

"And for Sheila," Crazy said.

Kasey saw the brotherhood in that moment, with Duke as their rock, and each one supporting each other.

Chip turned her toward him, and she stared into his eyes. "I've got to go, babe."

She didn't get the chance to say anything as the sound of cars approaching filled the air. Through the crowd of bikes and people, she wasn't able to see who it was.

"Diaz, what are you doing here?" Duke asked.

The man now known as Diaz to her shook Raoul's hand, and moved toward Duke. "My crew is your crew."

"This is not your fight."

"Trojans and my crew go back a long way. I'm not going to sit back. We've got your back. We're brothers, Duke, and I'm not going to let anything happen to you."

Duke and Diaz shook hands and did that man hug thing which seemed to be so popular.

Chip cupped Kasey's face, slamming his lips

down on hers. "You better keep your bed warm for me, baby."

He straddled his bike, and she stepped away.

"Everything is going to be okay."

One by one, the men climbed onto their bikes, and she couldn't believe the sight as one by one, they pulled out of the clubhouse.

She watched as Mary hugged Holly, the friendship shining between the two.

"It'll be fine," Holly said.

"Yeah, it will be fine. They're going to kick ass," Mary said.

Kasey still stared at the open gate, waiting, hoping that he would come back. She loved him, and she'd watched him ride off.

What if she didn't see him again?

Don't think like that.

He'll come back.

Recalling her brother's death, Kasey no longer felt in the mood for company, and so she reached into her purse, grabbing her keys.

Holly stepped in front of her. "He'll be back."

"I know. I've, erm, I've got to get to work. I'll call you guys."

Moving toward her car, she climbed inside, needing the peace away from it all. Knowing she loved Chip, and he was entering something so dangerous that it required all of the club, she was struggling.

Instead of going straight to work though, she drove the distance to where her brother rested with her parents. She hadn't been to his resting place in so long. Parking her car, she didn't care that it was so early as she made her way inside the dreary graveyard.

It had been a long time since she'd last been here, and moving toward the back of the graveyard, she stared down at the three stones that marked her family.

Her mother, Isabella Lintel.

Her father, Geoffrey Lintel.

Her brother, Shamus Lintel.

Three people that she had lost.

"Please, I don't know if there's a God, or if I even believe anymore, but please, take care of him and the club. Please."

Resting her head in her hands, she sat there for thirty minutes, just trying to find the peace that wouldn't come.

Finally, she went to the hospital to do her shift for the day.

****

Chip finished filling up his tank, and made his way inside the gas station picking up a couple bags of chips. They'd made a stop on the drive toward Abelli, who lived a couple of hours from Vale Valley.

Once he paid for his gas, he moved his bike out of the way, to allow for another to use the pump.

Opening his bag of cheese chips, he took a bite and sent a text to Kasey.

Chip: Eating some chips while waiting for the guys to fill up. How r u?

"How are you? Are you a pussy or something?" Pie asked.

Pocketing his cell phone, he took out another chip, shoving it into his mouth. He crushed the bag to his chest when Pie went to grab a chip.

"Tight ass."

"You bet ya." He turned, showing off his firm ass. "And this one doesn't share."

Pie stared at him for a few moments. "Kasey's good for you."

Chip stared at him, waiting to see if he'd joke

about it, or say some shit.

Eating another chip, he watched as Pie stood next to him, and they both stared at the gas station and the bikers filling up.

"You regret letting her go?" Chip asked.

"Nope. If I really wanted her, you wouldn't have stood a chance." Pie looked at him, "I don't share or give anyone a chance to take what's mine."

"I guess you don't."

"She's a good woman, though. I can see why you like her. She's one of a kind, a keeper."

Unable to resist, Chip offered Pie a chip; instead he took a large handful of them.

"You better have washed your hands," Chip said. He finished off the bag, tossing the wrapper into the trash and opening another.

Glancing at his cell phone he saw she hadn't texted him, and saw the time. He figured she'd gone to the hospital.

"Do you think they're happier?" Pie asked.

"Who?"

"The brothers who have settled for one pussy. Duke, Pike, all of them?"

"I've settled for one pussy."

"You've not made it official."

"I did. She's my old lady, and we'll talk about everything else when we get back."

"Kasey doesn't strike me as the kind of woman who'll be fucked in front of a bunch of men."

Chip glared at him. "Everything will be fine. Mary did it. Holly. All of the old ladies have been able to handle it. Kasey can handle it, too."

"Do you think it was Russ's way of getting a hard-on? Getting the chance to see all of the women?" Pie asked.

He looked at Pie. "No, I don't. He did it to show the difference between the club pussy and the old ladies."

The ceremony for an old lady required several of the club brothers to be present when the member claimed his old lady. The club accepted them as a union, and would risk their lives for the old lady, and she was not up for grabs. No one could make a play for her.

Now, a woman who wanted to become club property, a club whore, or a sweet-butt was taken by more than one man, and they had a train of fucking. The open invitation to more than one man to show there was no *one* claim. She wasn't an old lady. She was free pussy.

To some the ceremony was unnecessary, but Chip understood it as he believed it created a difference between the two types of women of the club.

Kasey was no sweet-butt. She was his woman, and he had no intention of sharing her with anyone.

"You think you're ever going to settle down?" Chip asked.

"Nah, I can't be done with settling down shit. There's way too much to enjoy right now, and I've no intention of ever letting one pussy control my dick. There's more than enough Pie to go around." Pie stood up. "Speaking of pie, I need a slice."

Chip smiled and rested against the wall, finishing his second bag of chips.

Landon came to stand with him. The brother looked troubled, and considering Landon often was the joker, that spoke volumes.

"What's got you looking like someone said your dick's rotten?"

"Just thinking."

"What about?"

"The meeting. What's going to happen."

"Take my advice, and don't think about it. Believe me, it'll drive you crazy. You don't need to keep thinking and worrying about that shit," Chip said.

"How?"

"Think about what you're looking forward to when you're done. I'm going to make Kasey my old lady, and then I'm going to either move in with her, or find a place a little closer. She lives too far from the clubhouse."

Landon laughed. "I like how you make these plans without even including her."

"I'm good like that. How are things with Maya?"

"Last night was rough. Knowing we were coming to visit her grandad, she didn't exactly sleep peacefully." Landon sighed. "Damn, I'm feeling really old right now."

"It happens to the best of us. Believe me." Chip's cell phone began to ring, and he checked the caller to see that it was his woman. "Duty calls." He stepped away, answering the call. "Hey, baby, miss me already?"

"Yeah, however the vomit was a close second."

"Vomit?"

"A drunk that couldn't keep it all down. I stink really bad. It's not attractive at all."

He wrinkled his nose. "I don't imagine it is."

"I won't be drinking vodka anytime soon."

"Nasty stuff."

"How is ... everything? The drive? Or is it the ride?"

"It's going great, baby. It'll be over before you know it. Are you going to the clubhouse after your shift?"

There were a few seconds of silence, and he waited.

"No. I'm going to head home. It's been a few

days since I hung out with Lindsey and she's complaining."

"Okay."

"Will you be home tonight?"

"Probably early tomorrow." He wanted to hold her, to kiss her, and tell her that everything was going to be okay.

"I went to my family's graveside today. Wow, that sounded morbid, didn't it?" she chuckled.

Now he wished he had her in his arms so that he could comfort her.

"I love you, Kasey."

"I love you, too. Come back to me, Rufus, please, come back."

His heart squeezed, and his gut twisted. "I will." The brothers were getting ready to leave. "I've got to head out. I'll call you when everything is done."

Hanging up his phone, he straddled his bike.

Chip wouldn't let her down.

****

Kasey made it to her apartment room floor when Lindsey came out of the room. Within a few feet of her Lindsey pressed her fingers over her nose. "Pee-yew, is that smell you?"

"Yep. I was urinated on, vomited on, and crapped on. Good times."

Lindsey kept a wide berth, and Kasey didn't even linger, going straight to her bathroom, where she removed her clothes, throwing them into the laundry basket. "Do you mind if I do the laundry first?"

"Nope. There's no way that smell can linger. I've closed your door," Lindsey said, entering the bathroom, and not seeming to care that Kasey was naked. She sprayed some lavender scented stuff in the air to hide the disgusting smell.

Turning her shower on, Kasey waited for the water to heat up, and climbed into the stall.

"We're still good for tonight, hanging out and having fun, or are you going to ditch me for cock?"

Kasey laughed. "Nope. No ditching today."

"Speaking of cock, where is your boyfriend?"

"Chip has a name."

"Yeah, well, I'm pissed at him."

Sticking her head out from the curtain, she stared at her neighbor. "Why?"

"He stole you from me."

"I'm not property," Kasey said.

"I know that, but I'm used to having you all to myself. I don't like to share, and I'm jealous."

She rolled her eyes. "You're still my friend. I'd have invited you to come to the clubhouse, but it's going through some really serious stuff at the moment."

"Drama?"

"Yep, and no, I can't gossip about it."

"Is this the kind of gossip that if you tell me, you'd have to kill me?" Lindsey asked.

"It's wrong that you sound excited about that, but yes. Seeing as I took a vow to do no harm, I really can't be killing you." She ran the soap all over her body, and even when the suds rinsed from her body, she was convinced she still smelled bad, so she did it all over again. "Tell me why you don't have your date, or one of your dates?"

"I'm not interested in screwing anyone right now."

"Why is that?" Kasey asked.

"I don't know. I guess I'm just bored of being disappointed. The past three men I've been with have been a real letdown, and you know what? I'm going to give myself time to actually want to screw again."

Putting the soap down, Kasey grabbed her shampoo, followed by her conditioner. Once she was completely rinsed off she was still sure she stank.

"Do I still stink?" Kasey asked.

"I can smell your clothes. Maybe that's what you can smell."

She turned the shower off, wrapping her body in the towel and opening the curtain. "I'm going to get dressed, and then I'm going to head down to the laundry room."

Lindsey followed her as she quickly changed into a pair of sweatpants, a bra, and large shirt.

The shirt was one of Chip's, and his scent surrounded her, calming her nerves, somewhat. They didn't disappear completely, but it also wasn't so bad either.

"You seem on edge," Lindsey said.

"Just dealing with some stuff right now." Not only had she admitted to falling in love with Chip to him, there was also the risk that he may not make it home alive, and apart from a talk earlier, she didn't know if he was all right. Grabbing her laundry basket, she waited outside for Lindsey as she grabbed hers.

"You know you can tell me anything, right? I won't judge."

"I know." They made their way down toward the basement area where the machines and driers were kept. She liked doing her laundry once a week, standing at the machines, folding, changing, and everything that it required. Instead of finding the job tedious, she actually found it really enjoyable. "I told Chip that I loved him."

"What did he say?"

"He told me he loved me first before I ever said anything."

"Why are you not like screaming, and happy

about this? And why didn't you tell me that Chip told you that he loved you?" Lindsey asked.

"I am. I am happy." Just thinking about it, a smile came to her lips. "I was kind of scared, actually."

"Why?"

"I've not known him that long, and then with everything going on, it just seemed a little fast. Do you think it's a little fast?"

"Do I think falling in love is real fast?"

"I don't know." They entered the laundry room, and Kasey went to the farthest machine and began to separate her clothes into different washes.

"Last time I checked, honey, there wasn't a time limit on how long it can take for you to fall in love with someone."

Putting the first load in the washing machine, she put the powder and softener inside, and started it up before helping Lindsey, who was taking way too long.

"Love is such a strong feeling, though."

"You can only know what you feel. When you look at Chip, what do you feel?" Lindsey asked.

"Like everything in the world is going to be okay, and nothing else can touch me. He makes everything better just by looking at him, and I couldn't imagine him not being in my life." The love she felt for him was absolute, but also the fear of knowing he could die today made her a little unsteady. She held onto the washing machine and was grateful for the support that Lindsey offered her.

"Are you okay?"

"I'm fine. I'm fine. It's just been a really long day." Between really difficult patients, constantly checking her cell phone, and just knowing something bad could happen, she was so tired.

"I thought I was in love once," Lindsey said.

"You were?"

"Yes. When I was in high school. It was the usual thing. The hottest guy in the world, you know. He made my heart go pitter-patter with just a look. I cannot believe I fell for him, but there was my luck. I fell for him so bad. It was … disgusting really, now that I think about it."

Kasey noticed that Lindsey got very busy, and her hands were shaking a little bit. It was the first time she'd ever seen the other woman in any way vulnerable.

"Anyway, he started being all nice to me, you know. Treating me like a princess, and saying all the nice things that girls want to hear. How pretty I am. How special I was to him. How he didn't give a fuck what anyone said because he loved me." Lindsey turned to her. "And so, I fell for him, and for a short time we were the weirdest couple in the world. I didn't care. I was so in love with him, and one night, I gave him my virginity. It wasn't great. It hurt a lot, and to be honest it was really boring, but that's the first time, right? Boring, painful, not exactly memorable. He filmed the entire experience with a hidden camera, and then uploaded it for everyone to see. It went all over social media. I pretty much had a sex video that went viral."

Kasey's heart went out to Lindsey.

Lindsey held her hands up. "It's okay. You don't need to hug me or anything. I don't need any sympathy. I fell for him, and he got me with the prank in the end. When I saw it, I had a breakdown in the toilet. Tears, snot, you name it. I think I even threw up. It had been a bet all along to get me into bed. That I would be so desperate for some attention, I'd throw myself at anyone. Anyway, after listening to a bunch of girls cackle at my expense, I was done being the one sitting in the toilet feeling ashamed, humiliated, and broken."

Kasey couldn't imagine that ever happening. She waited, listening as Lindsey continued to finish her story.

"I left the toilet. Held my head high. It suddenly occurred to me that not only had I fucked the most popular guy in school, the experience was awful, and just because he thought he'd gotten one over on me, I wasn't done. Of course, everyone thought I was the butt of the joke, but I decided that it wasn't going to end like that. I guess in a way my fuck 'em and leave 'em attitude began that day."

"Okay, now I'm curious. What did you do?" Kasey asked.

The wicked smile on Lindsey's face confirmed that she didn't take it lying down.

"I walked into the cafeteria, head high, instead of crying the whole time, and having lots of tears and puffy eyes. I'd stopped crying and splashed water on my face, so I probably looked like the most calm and collected girl in the entire school." She flicked her hair over her shoulder. "The cafeteria went so quiet as I looked for him. Now, up until this point, I'd been told what an amazing kisser I was. He was so shocked by how much he loved it when I kissed him. Anyway, instead of going to him, I walked right up to his friend, grabbed his face, and kissed him. I put my all into it. At first, he didn't respond, and then he did, and when I say he responded, he pulled me into his lap, and I felt the hard-on he was sporting. By the time we finished I asked him if he was better in the sack than his loser friend. By the end of the afternoon, no one was laughing at me. They were laughing at him as the video also showed how lame he was in bed."

"Wow," Kasey said. "Only you can go and kiss the next guy. Did you know you were going to do that?"

"I didn't have a clue to be honest. I entered that

cafeteria, and I got so angry. I just reacted, and I wanted no part in it. Besides, within a few weeks we graduated, and I was done. I never slept with anyone else at the school."

Kasey pulled her into her arms. "I'd have crushed his balls for you."

Lindsey laughed. "You can't even hurt a fly, so I'll be the one doing all that ball-crushing you keep on talking about."

"Very true." With Lindsey talking to her, one of the washes had finished.

She realized that she'd been distracted for twenty minutes while her clothes washed.

"Thank you," she said.

"You're very welcome."

They continued to do their washing as Lindsey kept on chattering away. Kasey loved listening to her friend, and what she had to say. Some of the stories made her laugh. Before too long, three hours had passed and she couldn't stand the wait anymore.

"I'm just going to make a call."

"Sure. I'll keep an eye on things."

Leaving the room, she sat down on the third step and held her cell phone in her hand. She didn't call Chip. The last thing she wanted to do was give him a distraction if he was in the middle of something, so she put a call to Holly, waiting anxiously as she answered.

"Hello," Holly said, a little out of breath.

"Hey, it's just me. I was wondering if you'd heard anything?"

"No, not yet. We're all here if you'd like to come and check. We all like to stay at the clubhouse when shit goes down."

She looked toward the room, hearing Lindsey hum. "It's okay. I've got company, and I really don't think I could handle being there right now."

"Okay. I'll call you if there's any change."

"Thank you. Is it normal to wait this long?"

"Yes. It is. I'm sorry I can't give you any more information."

"It's fine."

Saying their goodbyes, Kasey hung up the phone.

Closing her eyes, she rested her head in her hands, taking several deep breaths. She didn't want to be dealing with this right now. She felt so utterly alone.

"Bad conversation?" Lindsey asked, peeking out the door.

"It wasn't bad, but it didn't exactly tell me what I wanted to hear."

"I'm a big girl if you want to go to the clubhouse and be with them."

"Nah, it's fine. I like being here. Spending time with you." She rubbed her friend's hand, and rested her head on Lindsey's shoulder. "I don't want anything to happen to him."

Lindsey didn't say anything. She put her arm around her shoulders and hugged her.

There really wasn't anything else she could do.

Chapter Eleven

Earlier in the day

When they were thirty minutes from Abelli territory, Duke flagged them all down near a parking zone. Pulling his bike inside, Chip turned off the ignition and moved to hear what Duke had to say.

"The moment we cross that line we'll be on Abelli's land. He'll know we're coming, and our element of surprise will be ruined."

Chip had already figured that out. This was just another reason why this was so dangerous. They could all be killed before they even got to Francis Abelli.

"If any of you want to turn around and head back, I will not under any circumstances hold it against you."

No one moved a muscle or even looked like they were going to.

"You've got kids and family," Duke said.

"So have you, Duke," Raoul said. "I'm not backing away. We end this today, and I am done playing this game."

Duke nodded. "You're all ready? I can't guarantee that we'll all make it out alive."

"For those that don't, take care of their families," Pike said. "Make sure they're taken care of."

Then they were back on their bikes and heading into Abelli turf. Chip smiled. He loved being on his bike, on the open road, and fuck it if this didn't feel so good, taking the fight to Abelli.

For a long time the Trojans MC hadn't dealt with any kind of shit storm like this. They'd been dealing their business, doing the normal kind of shit. Fucking, falling in love, the runs that Ned Walker arranged for them. Then Maya came to them, followed by the truth about

Holly. It had been like a noose tied around their necks, waiting for the stool beneath them to be pushed out.

No more.

They were not a club that had death waiting for them. They were the club that brought death to whoever threatened it, and he was done waiting.

As he rode toward the Francis Abelli mansion, Chip's rage grew with every passing second. He thought about Holly, about Russ and Sheila, and also about the love he had for Kasey. If he didn't make it, he'd be so pissed, but he'd also put everything in place with the club so that she would be taken care of if anything happened to him.

He didn't want it to go that way.

As he rode toward his possible death, he thought about everything he wanted to do. To take Kasey on the back of his bike, to date her, to show her the love he felt building inside him, and the life he wanted with her.

Not only did he want to claim her as his old lady, but he also wanted to marry her for real. For her to take his hand and for them to walk together as one. He wanted to get her pregnant and to see her swollen with his kid. Just the thought made his dick ache, and when he got home, he was going to tell her what he wanted, how much he loved her, and that no matter what he would make her happy.

The gates were open when they got to Abelli's land, and they rode right inside. Diaz had pulled away, and Chip figured they'd come in when they needed it, or they liked the scenery.

He really didn't give a shit. Parking his bike along the line of Trojans MC, Duke took the lead just as Francis Abelli along with all of his men came out of the house.

"Well, I have to say to what do I owe this little

surprise?" Francis Abelli asked.

Chip looked at Abelli's goons, checking out the ones on the outer edge and seeing that they looked the most collected of all of them.

They all had a hand on their guns, and the crew did as well. Chip held his gun ready to take aim.

"Well, you see, I have a little problem. I thought we were all friends here. You know. I'm with your granddaughter, and we had a deal that Anton ended everything between us," Duke said, stepping forward.

Chip didn't take his gaze off Francis, whose eye had twitched at the mention of his son.

"We did," Francis said. His voice no longer sounded like the cheery fellow of moments ago.

"You see, I thought that." Duke began to pace, walking several steps ahead, then turning and walking back. "Let me get this entirely straight. Anton wanted either Sheila and Russ, and there was no chance in hell of me giving over any of my club or my club women. So I come to you, and you guarantee to me that you'll keep your son in line. I won't go into the entire detail of that conversation as you were there. We had that conversation, you and I, and you told me Anton would be taken care of. So in *my* own parking lot, in *my* clubhouse." Duke had stopped at this point, and was poking his chest with each time he said "my." He'd stopped pacing. "Sheila and Russ were taken from us. Two people you swore to me would be safe were killed in *my* house, on *my* land."

Francis's jaw clenched.

"You see, Francis, buddy, pal. That's two people you couldn't even fucking protect. Being the good guy that I am, I decided that instead of taking out two of your guys, I took out your very troublesome son. Believe me, I can count. Two to one, you were getting the better fucking deal. Not only did I have to bury two of my people, I've had to deal with the fucked-up shit that was done to my wife. You know, the mother of my children. Which is fine. I can handle that. I can handle having to be the big man, and take care of my wife when she's lost her parents. The two people she saw as her parents in the world." Duke moved toward his cool box, lifting it off the back of the bike.

Guns were pulled out and aimed, the tension increasing with every passing second.

Francis held out his hand, keeping his men at bay.

"So you see, Francis, I'm a bit confused. We agreed that Anton was the end of it. No one else would die. You'd back off. I'd back off, and we'd both enjoy our fucking back-off party, when this piece of shit turns up."

The head of the man asking a lot of questions was pulled out by his hair, and tossed toward Abelli.

Chip held his gun steady, watching the men, making sure no one got a shot off. None of them were taking out his Prez.

He wondered what the fuck Diaz was doing.

Duke threw the cool box to the ground. "Now tell me what the fuck that is?"

Francis stared at the head on the floor then looked up.

Silence fell between them.

It stretched for several moments, and Duke's hands were on his hips, waiting.

"You made a mistake coming here," Abelli said, the first one to cave.

Duke shook his head. "Nah, I didn't make a mistake. I'm not the one that backed out of our deal. You did. The way I see it, a life for a life. This fucker, that makes three." Suddenly Duke took out his gun and fired at the first man in the long line of men. Still Abelli didn't move a hand. "Now we're even."

Francis smiled. "Do you really think you're going to leave here alive?"

Duke laughed, and it took Francis by surprise. "You really think I give a shit? You really think that I'd take my men on a suicide mission without guaranteeing their safety? I'm not you, Francis Abelli. You pushed the wrong man. I'm not Russ. I'm not one of your pussy goons. I won't be pushed around." Duke turned toward them. "I'm Duke. The infamous Prez of the Trojans MC, and no one messes with us."

Abelli gave the signal just as Diaz and his crew made his way out of the house.

Gunshots rang out, and Chip cried out as pain exploded in his leg. He held his gun out, firing at the fucker that had got a bullet inside him. He'd been so intent on watching fucking Abelli that he'd not seen the fucker aim toward him, and now he was so fucking pissed off.

The pain was instant, and it burned.

One by one, Abelli's men went down. Chip gripped the wound in his leg, fucked off that he'd been shot. He'd not been shot in a long time, and now he was angry. He wanted to go home looking like a hero to his woman, and now that he'd been shot, there was no way in hell that was happening, which pissed him off.

Minutes passed, and Chip stayed in position, gun poised. The only man standing was Francis Abelli.

"You bastard," Francis said.

Diaz held a knife to his throat. He kicked him, sending Francis down to his knees, and Duke walked up to him.

"I think my parents were married, so I'm not much of a bastard." Duke took the blade from Diaz, nodding at him. "Never invite a Trojan horse into your house, Francis. You don't know what they're hiding. Didn't the myths ever tell you the truth?"

Chip watched as Duke held the blade at Francis Abelli's throat. Then Duke slid it across Francis's neck, blood spilled, and he gurgled before falling dead at Duke's feet.

Silence rang out, and Chip looked at the carnage in front of them.

Duke was doing the same, looking at the large building, then at the bodies. "Torch it."

"You don't want to take some souvenir?" Pike asked.

"No. I don't want anything this fucker touched. I made a statement. That's all I wanted to do." Duke shook Diaz's hand. "Thank you."

"That's what I'm here for."

"Let's have a damage count," Duke said.

"Chip, Floss, and Daisy have been shot, but other than that, we're all perfectly fine," Pike said.

"Speak for yourself, it fucking burns," Floss said.

"Yeah, I can't claim this is fucking easy or a picnic. How the fuck am I going to get home?" Chip asked.

Pie came toward him. "It's a flesh wound. You can ride bitch for me." Pie ran a hand down his face, and Chip slapped his hand away.

The building was torched, and Chip was riding bitch for Pie, which really pissed him off. Diaz packed the bikes that they couldn't ride in the back of their vehicles. Chip was so pissed off that he'd been shot. They'd put a tourniquet to help stop the bleeding. He couldn't go to a hospital, so he had to get home.

He hoped Kasey wasn't angry at him.

****

Kasey opened her eyes, groaning as she realized she slept with Lindsey. Her cell phone was vibrating, and she reached out, grabbing it. It had been a couple of hours, and she must have passed out on her sofa.

She saw it was Holly's name, and sitting up, wiping her eyes, she answered it.

"Hey, do you know anything?"

"They're back, Kasey. They're all back, but erm, Chip, he … got shot. He's asking for you."

Pushing Lindsey's legs off her, Kasey was up. "I'll be right there. I'm coming."

Her heart racing, she quickly checked to make sure she looked fine. Lindsey woke up with a groan.

"That's not a nice way to wake a woman, shoving her legs off you."

"I'm so sorry. I've got to head out though. I can't stay and linger."

"What?"

"Chip's back, and I want to go and check on him. It's nothing personal. You can stay here, and I'll bring you breakfast or lunch or something," Kasey said.

She hugged Lindsey and rushed out the door.

Kasey didn't wait for the elevator. She rushed down the stairs, leaving her apartment block and climbing in the car.

Within minutes she was on the road, heading toward the clubhouse. She broke speed limits to get there in record time.

She parked her car with a screech, which she didn't care about. Running into the clubhouse, she saw Holly.

"Where is he?" she asked.

"He's down in the basement. The doctor is with him."

Following Holly, she saw several of the brothers,

including Pie.

"Hey, baby," Chip said.

The doctor moved out of the way, and Kasey sobbed, rushing toward him, wrapping her arms around him.

He held her tightly, and she cupped his face, kissing him.

"I was so worried. So scared that something went wrong, that something happened to you."

"Nothing happened to me, baby. I'm fine. I'm alive and well."

She stroked a finger down his cheek and laughed. "I missed you."

"I missed you, too. You're going to have to take care of me, though."

Kasey realized he wasn't wearing any pants, and his leg was bandaged up. "What happened?"

"One of the perps got me, baby."

"Oh, no." She saw that it was completely clean, and the bandage looked right. "Does it hurt?"

"Yes, it hurts." He sat up, and moved so that he was about to stand. "Will you help me upstairs? I don't want to lie down here all night."

He put one arm around her shoulders, and she helped him leave the basement. She was so happy right now that he was alive, and well, and he was more than fine.

It took her some time to help him up to his room, and Pie finally conceded and helped.

"I could lift you up in my arms, and totally carry you like the hero in a movie."

"Fuck off, Pie," Chip said.

"Or I could drop you and your heavy ass," Pie said.

"Don't you dare," she said. "Don't hurt him."

"As the lady wishes."

She pulled back the bedsheets, and Chip lay down. "I think it's safe to say I need a few days' rest," he said with a groan.

"Anything you need, give me a shout," Pie said.

"Thank you."

Closing the door, Kasey rushed toward him, moving onto the other side of the bed and kissing him, over and over.

"I take it you were worried."

"I didn't want anything to happen to you. I've been so worried all day. I … I don't even want to think of anything else right now. I just want to be happy that you made it out of there alive."

Chip stroked her cheek.

"Is the danger gone?" she asked.

"Yeah, the danger is gone. Duke had everything under control. I should never doubt that son of a bitch."

She laughed.

"Why are you crying?" he asked.

"I'm so happy. I don't want anything to happen to you, and if I had any doubts about being in love with you, I know they're unfounded. I love you so much, Chip. It kind of scares me how much. I'm not used to feeling this way."

Chip smiled. "I love you as well, baby. So much. All I could think about was getting home to you, loving you. There's so much I want to do with you, baby. I want us to build a life together."

"I want that as well. I don't care that it has only been a matter of weeks, but I can't lose you. This was too close for me."

"I know."

He pushed some of her hair off her shoulder, and his gaze moved to her mouth then up to her eyes. "I want you to marry me," he said.

"Marry?"

"Yes, marry. I want you to marry me. I want us to have a family. That's not going to change."

"You know, I'm not going to say no, but I think before we make plans for a life together, we really should get you well."

"I'll hold you to that."

Kasey snuggled close to him, feeling at peace for the first time in her life, or at least, since she'd lost her brother.

"You know, it's just my leg that's injured. My dick is more than fine," Chip said.

She burst out laughing. "A bullet won't keep you down, will it?"

"Nothing is going to keep me down."

Chapter Twelve

Chip made his recovery last as long as possible. He loved having Kasey wait on him, and she also took some time off in the early days after his injury to attend to his wound and his every single need.

Providing the bedroom door was locked, she'd sit on the bed, completely naked, legs spread, playing cards. The first time he asked, they hadn't closed the door, and Pie had walked in to bring them a drink.

Kasey had dived over the other side of the bed to hide herself, and he'd thrown pillow after pillow at the man's face to get him the fuck out of his room.

Of course, Pie kept trying to make excuses, but Kasey kept the door locked at all times.

Finally, after a month of care, and with no way at all for him to prolong the wound, the doctor told everyone he'd been good to party for a long time.

On that Friday night, he sat on the edge of the bed watching as Kasey got ready to go for a girls' night out.

Landon had agreed to be their driver, and Chip didn't want her to go. She looked so sexy wearing a dress that hugged her curves, and made him ache to fuck her brains out.

"I can't believe you told a little lie. You were well all along," Kasey said. "Be honest, when did you start to feel better?"

"Around the second week but I loved your attention, and you spent a lot of time doing what I wanted. So please stay home, and I can totally make you forget your name." He took her hand, pulling her close.

"Nope, not going to happen. I've put off girls' night because you were injured. I'll keep an eye on our pregnant girls, Zoe and Mary." She kissed his lips. "But I really want to be there tonight to have some fun. You know, I don't think I've ever gone out with the girls before. This will be a brand new experience for me."

Chip stood and stroked her cheek. She wore a little makeup, some lipstick, but no foundation.

To him, she didn't need the enhancement of beauty products. When she got home tonight he was going to tell her truth about the old lady claiming. He'd been putting it off as he didn't want her to be pissed or worse, not agree to do it.

There was a knock, and Lindsey entered the room. "Come on, girlfriend, I want to go and party. Hey, little liar. Feeling okay?"

Lindsey had taken to calling him "little liar" and other little names that were digs at him keeping Kasey with him for longer.

"I'm more than okay. You'll keep an eye on my girl tonight?"

"Totally. I'm going to make sure she dances with guys who run their hands all over her body."

Chip pulled Kasey against him.

"I'm kidding, mister possessive. We're going to have fun, dance, and I've taken a vow of no men, so that means all of them will be over me."

Kasey laughed. "How do you figure that out?"

"It's karma, right? I say I don't want a man, so I'll find my perfect man. With you and Chip being all loved up and making plans, I want that. I want to find a guy to love me for me, and screw everyone else, and everything else." She flicked her hair over her shoulder.

Chip watched her leave his room, and he followed Kasey downstairs to where the other old ladies were waiting. He quickly saw that several of the club brothers were not impressed with this girls' night out either.

"You could have your girls' night here," Duke said.

"Not going to happen," Holly said. "Don't wait up."

Chip moved out toward the waiting car. Kasey climbed into the back seat, and Landon took the wheel. The girls can drink, but the pregnant women couldn't.

He watched them go, and looked toward Pike and Duke. "Any of you wanting to follow them?"

"We do, but we can't do it. They'll make our lives hell," Pike said.

"How do you figure?" Chip asked.

"They go out on girls' night every once in a while. We start to make a big deal out of it, and they'll make it every single week," Duke said. "So just go sit on your ass, drink a beer, and wait until she comes back."

The men slapped him on the back. Seeing no reason to worry, he followed the brothers inside, taking the beer that Pie offered him.

"Are you hanging in there?" Pie asked.

He glared at Pie, who held his hands up.

"Go easy on me. I'm not the one that said yes to your girl going out. That was all you, and I had nothing to do with it."

"You're just jealous that I got the girl," Chip said, smirking.

"Nah, there's plenty of pussy. I didn't want her after all, and I'm certainly not pining or anything." Pie grabbed his dick. "I'm too good to fall for one woman."

"You keep on saying that," Duke said. "There's going to be a woman for you before you know it."

Chip sipped at his beer. Pie was way too confident. A woman was going to make Pie fall, and when that happened, he wanted to be there to see it.

****

"So do the guys know about the male strippers?" Kasey asked, taking a sip of her cocktail. She didn't even know what it was called, just that it was nice and fruity. She'd never been out with the girls.

Holly finished off one cocktail and ordered another.

Mary looked toward the male strippers and shrugged. "I don't really come here for the eye candy. Mine is at home, and I can touch without having to put a dollar in his pants. Pike will dance for me for free."

"It's not so bad," Zoe said, sitting back. "They look a little … clean. I know they're slicked in some kind of body oil, but there's no ink, and they're so pretty and perfect."

"Raoul's pretty and perfect," Holly said.

"Yeah, but he's got ink and that badass vibe. I'm just not into the whole good boy thing. Give me my bad boy any day," Zoe said, rubbing her stomach.

"And now you've got your own bad boy," Lindsey said to Kasey. "I've seen the way Chip looks at you, and there's no mistaking how much he loves you. My girl is totally loveable." Lindsey rested her head on Kasey's shoulder.

"I really do like you," Mary said, pointing at Lindsey. "It's refreshing to have a woman without a filter."

"I can't keep crap to myself. I tell it how it is. I'll be back with another round." Lindsey jumped up and took their empty glasses.

An upbeat song began to play, and Holly took the lead, going to the dance floor. Being part of the circle, Kasey danced with all the women, finally letting go and relaxing.

Lindsey brought their drinks to the table, and they all sat around sipping. Mary and Zoe had sodas while the rest enjoyed cocktails.

Landon kept a good distance away, and Kasey saw he was reading a book, which she found so cute.

"He's not going to join in?" she asked the table.

"Nope. He always catches up on his reading when we have girls' night. He's the only one that offers to be our chauffeur for the night. He's such a good guy," Zoe said.

She knew from Chip that Landon and Zoe were best friends and had gone to college together.

Protecting Zoe had earned Landon his patch along with many other jobs he'd done.

The night wore on, and between drinking cocktails, dancing, and eating some potato chips that came with the service, Kasey was buzzing. Tomorrow she would totally have a headache, but that was okay.

She had the day off, and she intended to spend it with her man. Just thinking about Chip filled her with so much love.

He was her man, and she was his woman.

Later that night, before they headed back to the clubhouse, Mary suggested they stop for Chinese. While they were there, cameras were out, taking selfies, which Holly and Mary said would go on their blog. Eating her way through a large pile of noodles, Kasey couldn't recall a time she'd felt so happy.

Lindsey excused herself, and Kasey stole a coconut fried shrimp.

"So, has Chip told you about taking you as his old lady?" Holly asked.

"He said that he needed to talk about it. He calls it a ceremony. I don't know. It's not that big of a deal." Holly slurped up her noodles, and looked around the table to see that all women were staring at her. "What? Do I have sauce on my chin?"

"Has he told you what happens during it?" Mary asked.

"No, we haven't talked about it. He says it's important, but I figure he'd tell me when he was ready." She shrugged. The look on their faces didn't make her feel so good though. "What?"

Holly sighed. "My mother told me. For the guys to claim an old lady in the eyes of the club, he has to have sex with you in front of several members. No one else touches—"

"Wait! What?"

Kasey listened as they told her how an old lady was claimed in the eyes of the club. "That's total … bullshit!"

"It's the club law," Holly said. "It's their way of making a distinction between a club whore that anyone can touch, and being an old lady. Several of the guys were there with mine, and they've not made me feel uncomfortable."

Kasey put down her chopsticks. "Have you all done it?"

"Yes."

She tapped her fingers on the table.

They had each become an old lady by being fucked while other men watched.

Biting her lip, she understood quite clearly why her man didn't tell her what it meant to become his old lady.

"This is a … surprise," she said.

"It's not that bad," Eliza, Brass's woman, said. "I found it to be quite erotic, actually."

"Duke doesn't like to share. Looking back, I see that it actually showed his very possessive side. No one else was allowed to touch me, but they knew I was his special lady," Holly said.

Lindsey came back from the bathroom, and any conversation about it ceased.

They finished their meal, and Landon waited in the car. He dropped Lindsey off, and her friend was so drunk that Kasey got out of the car, asking for them to keep it running. She helped her friend home and climbed back into the car.

There was no way she wanted to wait to become Chip's old lady. She was a little drunk, but she couldn't wait another day.

She ignored the conversation going on around her and focused instead on the road ahead. Her thoughts all over the place as she thought of Chip and what they were going to have to do.

It was … stupid.

Screwing women in front of the club just sounded so lame, but it kind of made sense. What she didn't like was that Holly had been the one to tell her, not her man.

Landon pulled into the clubhouse parking lot. Kasey didn't wait around to see if Chip came out. Entering the clubhouse, she went straight to him. The smile on his face when he saw her didn't stop her from going to him.

He stood up by the time she stepped close to him. Staring up the length of his body, she was once again taken by the pure maleness of him. Licking her dry lips, she forced that to the back of her mind, and thought about right now.

"I want you to make me your old lady," she said.

"What?"

"You heard me. Holly's told me the truth of how it happens, and even though I'm a little upset for you not telling me, I want you do it. Right now, tonight. I'm your old lady, and I'm never going to step out on you, or rat on the club. I don't even know all the terms, but I'm loyal, Chip. I love you, and I'm a loyal person. There's no one else I want, and if you want me to be your old lady, then you'll do that right now, tonight. I can't wait another second."

His gaze moved past her shoulder, and she looked behind her to see Holly and Duke there.

Several of the guys nodded, and she returned her attention to Chip.

He stepped toward her, cupping her face. "You're a little drunk."

"I'm not drunk. A little tipsy maybe, but I want this. I want you, and there's no way I'm going to be backing away from this. I want you, and I believe you want me."

"There's no doubt about that."

Kicking off her heels, she wrapped her arms around his neck, pulling his head down. She kissed him hard, moaning as his tongue traced across her lips. The lipstick she'd worn earlier had long gone, and he tasted of chocolate and beer.

Slowly, he moved her back, and she didn't let go of him.

All of her life she'd been able to zone out everything that distracted her. Years of being a student had perfected that, so she focused on Chip. She didn't think of Pie, Duke, Holly, Raoul, Zoe, Bertie, Floss, or the others as they sat down.

He lifted her up, dropping her down onto the pool table, and she noticed he did it so she couldn't see anyone but him.

"I don't want anyone to see what belongs to me, and I also don't want you getting ideas of being with someone else. You're mine, Kasey."

"Yes, I'm yours. I'll always be yours, and nothing is going to change that."

He took possession of her mouth, and she moaned as his hands moved up her thighs, taking the skirt with him as he pushed it to her waist. She lifted up a little, and he tore her panties off, pocketing them.

His hands went to her breasts, cupping them. Fire ignited inside her, and she couldn't believe how aroused he was making her, especially with their audience.

Ignoring that, though, she kept her gaze on him, not wanting anyone, or anything else.

"Fuck, I love you, baby, you have no idea how much."

She cupped his face, kissing him back. "Take me, Chip."

He opened the zipper of his pants, unbuttoning it, pulling out his length. She wrapped her fingers around his dick, running her thumb across the tip, relishing his moan as she worked him.

"Fuck, baby, that feel so fucking good."

She couldn't agree more. It *did* feel good. Being his woman always felt so good.

Chip was already rock hard, and when he pushed her back just a little, spreading her thighs, he teased the tip across her clit before sliding down.

Her pussy was slick from his touch alone.

He pushed the first couple of inches inside her, gripped her hips, and slammed the rest deep inside her core.

She cried out his name as his cock stretched her pussy. He reached between them, sliding his finger back and forth, drawing her closer to orgasm.

"I want you to come on my cock, baby. When you do, I'll fuck you, and you'll be mine."

He used two fingers to stroke her clit, and she gasped with each flick across her nub, which set her on fire for more. She didn't want him to stop, and he didn't, not until he made her come.

Her pleasure echoed off the walls, and Chip didn't hold back in claiming her. He fucked her hard, consuming her.

Everything else fell away, and they became the only two people that mattered in the world. He drove her crazy, and she basked in his touch. The fire he started filled every part of her heart and soul. There was no coming down from the peak, and when he came, they didn't linger. Chip pulled out of her pussy, and the dress fell down to her thighs.

They rushed out of the main room and he took her to his, closing and locking the door.

He pinned her up against the door, holding her in place. "I just fucked you without a condom."

"I know." She felt his cum leaking from her pussy.

"I want you to have my babies. I want you to be my wife. I want ... everything with you."

"That's a lot of wants."

"Don't be angry with me for not telling you."

"I'm not angry."

"Don't be disappointed either."

"I'm not disappointed," she said. "Actually, I'm a *little* disappointed, but I tend to get over that really fast. Just don't hide anything like that from me again."

"The first time I met you, I had no idea just how much you'd come to mean to me."

"When did we first meet?"

"When Leanna was in the hospital. I passed you on the stairs, and asked you where I could find her. You gave me directions."

She frowned. "I can't remember that?"

"It was a long time ago. A whole other life. You were marking stuff on your chart."

"Who would have thought in that moment I'd be your old lady, and you'd be proposing marriage to me."

"I sure didn't," he said. "I thought you were beautiful. I did recognize that about you."

"Well then everything is more than fine if I looked pretty enough for you." She chuckled, and he picked her up, carrying her toward the bed.

"Now, I get to make love to you in every single way that matters."

Chapter Thirteen

One month later

"This is the one," Chip said.

"You think so?" Kasey asked.

They'd been hunting for a place to stay together. He didn't want to stay in Kasey's apartment, and wanted to make a life together. In the past three weeks they'd seen sixteen apartments and ten houses. He was tired of seeing other people's shit and trying to imagine a life for himself in that property.

"This is an excellent home. Very good for starting a family," the real estate agent said. He didn't catch the woman's name.

Taking Kasey's hand, he moved her toward the kitchen where a window looked over the garden, with the sink in front of them.

Moving her so that she was in front of him, he wrapped his arms around her. "I want you to imagine standing here, washing dishes, as I know you love doing that. I'm out there. Our son, our daughter, both, or two sons or two daughters, and we're laughing, playing around." He kissed her neck.

"You paint a great picture."

He knew they weren't pregnant yet, but he hoped one day soon he'd hit it just right. "This is our family. Lindsey can visit us anytime, and you're closer to the hospital."

"You're closer to the clubhouse."

"It's got three bedrooms."

"You want two kids?"

"To start," he said. "I don't want to scare you. I just want to build a family. A life with you. An apartment is not ever going to cut it. You know that."

She sighed. "You're really pushing here."

He laughed, and turned to the agent. "We'll take it."

"That's excellent. This will bring you many happy years, of that I can guar—"

Chip tuned her out, and rested his chin on Kasey's shoulder. "What are you thinking, babe?"

"I'm thinking that this is going to be a really nice house, and I also noticed that there's no furniture already here, and that we could start moving in soon."

"That's what I was thinking as well. The guys don't do shit anymore, so I'll get them started on loading the trucks."

He linked their fingers together, and he teased the band of her engagement ring. Their wedding was also being prepared for as they spoke.

To help Mary and Holly with their blog after there was such a long time without any interaction at all, they were hosting a biker's special wedding. It would be at the clubhouse, and the two women were arranging everything from flowers, to the food, and decorations. Kasey got to have her say at least, and he liked that.

"You know, I was thinking there could be a few times you could do the dishes, and I could go and play with the kids," she said, laughing.

"That would work. You could be in a bikini, and I could watch you walking around the garden, your tits bouncing with every single step you took."

She threw her head back, laughing. "Your mind is always in the gutter."

"Always, and you love it. We're going to need to figure out baby names."

"Already? I'm not even pregnant."

"I like to plan ahead. I'm thinking Neil for a boy, and Nell for a girl."

Kasey shook her head. "That's not going to happen. Not now. Not ever." She cupped his face, kissing him. "I hate to cut this short, but you really need to take me home. I've got to finish my shift."

"I can't wait until you're on maternity leave."

"I've cut back some of my hours."

It still wasn't enough. He never got enough time with her, and he hated that.

Driving back to the hospital, he waited for her to go inside the doors before texting the guys to get started.

He'd already purchased the house they'd gone to see that day. He'd stopped by three days ago with Pie, and he'd paid extra to pay the deposit, and to get the real estate to play along with the purchase.

Driving back to the house, he saw the guys were already unloading furniture to his place.

"You don't think she's going to be a little pissed about us doing all of this for you?" Duke asked.

"She won't. She'll love it."

Lindsey was with them, and helped get all of Kasey's clothes hung up in the open closet.

Within a matter of hours, the club had helped him turn an empty house into their home, and as he looked around, he just knew without a shadow of a doubt that she was going to love it here with him.

Later that day, when he went to pick her up he discovered his answer was indeed right. Kasey loved the house.

"I can't believe it! How? When?"

"I saw this place a few days ago when you were at work. I stood at the kitchen sink where we were, and I just knew this was going to be our place, that you'd love it."

"And if I hadn't?"

"Then I was going to have to pull out of the deal.

The guy that was selling it was more than happy to speed things along. He wanted rid of the house, and I wanted the house for myself. It was a win-win." He pulled her into his arms, kissing her lips.

She kissed him back with a passion that stirred his cock. "You know those flowers you got me were so amazing, but I think you've outdone yourself with this house."

"You think so?"

"I know so."

Picking her up in his arms, he carried her upstairs to their bedroom and made love to her throughout the night.

****

Pie sat on the wall of the parking lot staring up at the clubhouse. A party was going on inside. Everyone was celebrating, and he was by himself, a cigarette in his mouth, and a bottle of whiskey in his hand.

Something wasn't right with him.

The club was fine. Abelli's potential threat was completely eliminated, and the Trojans MC's reputation remained intact.

He'd helped Chip move in with Kasey, and he was just … alone. Miserable.

"You know for a guy who is known for the life of the party, you're sure being miserable," Lindsey said, coming out of the house.

"Yeah, so why are you here to join me?"

She sat on the wall and stared over at the clubhouse. "I can see why you love it here."

"Why don't you join?"

"Not a chance. Don't get me wrong, I love sex as much as the next person, but being a sweet-butt, being passed around from one guy to the next—I have my limits." She held her hand up. "Besides, I like being around the old ladies, and in case you didn't notice, they rarely speak with the girls who offer free pussy."

He burst out laughing.

Lindsey was a hoot.

"Again, why are you out here alone?"

"Just thinking."

"Is this because Chip and Kasey are settling down?"

"Nope. I knew I didn't stand a chance with her."

"Stop lying. You're really not that great at bullshitting, just so you know. You're pretty terrible at it. The worst."

Pie took a swig of whiskey, offering it to his companion, and she waved her head, telling him no.

"What makes you think I'm bullshitting?" he asked.

"You don't strike me as the kind of guy who buys flowers for women and doesn't expect something. You liked Kasey. Probably didn't love her, but you liked her."

"So?"

"So, don't pretend you didn't. It's lame."

He stared at the clubhouse, and sighed. Lindsey was a nice woman. No filter, and a little too much at times, but she was easy to talk to.

"This bullshit stays between us," he said.

"Totally. I don't share secrets."

He took a deep breath. "I want what the guys have."

"I guess we're talking about what the married guys have, right?"

"Yes. I want that."

Lindsey sighed. "Why were you bragging about wanting all the pussy and not settling for just one?"

"How do you know about that?"

"I have ears, and you say it often. You say it

enough so that you can believe it." She took the whiskey from him, gulping it down. "Then we need to get you a woman."

"Yeah, like that's ever going to happen."

"I'm serious. We have dating sites nowadays. I'm sure there's a woman out there for you, who'll make your dreams come true."

Pie stared at her, waiting. "What's the catch?"

Lindsey smiled. "That you will help me find my dream man, too. I'm totally off men, so dating is the key. I want to find Mr. Right." She held her hand out. "Do we have a deal?"

"We've got a deal." He shook her hand, hoping he'd not made the biggest mistake of his life.

****

Three weeks later

Kasey had arranged for some vacation time, and was determined to spend it all with Chip. She hoped she didn't drive him crazy as she'd already changed the whole house. What the guys at the club did had been amazing, and she loved them all for it, but for it to be a home, she had to have her own touch. She just had to.

So, the living room now looked comfortable instead of just a bunch of furniture dumped in. The kitchen had order, and the dining room looked ready for guests.

Lindsey had to have been the one to set out her closet because that was a nightmare. Kasey liked to have neatness, order, so jeans in a row, followed by skirts, shirts, then dresses. Not mish-mashed all over the place.

It didn't matter now.

Order was in place, and she was happy.

"Okay, so what is the big emergency that you couldn't wait two minutes while I showered?" Chip asked, leaving the house.

She smiled at him. His hair was damp, reminding her exactly how good he looked naked and fucking her.

Put those thoughts to bed.

She wanted to go to bed, but later.

"I was wondering…" She bit her lip, knowing it drove him crazy. "I don't mean to assume anything, but would you give me a ride? There's someone I'd like you to meet."

When he moved toward the car, she stopped him. She stood right beside his bike. "No, not in the car," she said. "I want you to take me for a ride on your bike."

"You've always asked not to go on that."

"I know, but I'd like you to take me on a ride." She gave him the location of where she wanted him to go.

He stood in front of her. "Are you sure about this?"

"Yes, I'm sure." Her love and trust in Chip were absolute. She couldn't imagine being with anyone else.

Chip held out the helmet for her.

"Oh, come on."

"Nope. You ride with me this first time, you're wearing the helmet."

She smiled as she put the helmet on. "You're a spoilsport."

"And there's no way that I'm risking the love of my life before I've even got a chance to marry her."

He climbed onto the bike, and she straddled his waist, wrapping her arms around him. The moment the machine purred to life, she didn't have any fear.

She just felt an overwhelming sense of love for her man. He took off, and she knew he was being cautious as they drove away from their house.

Chip began to gather speed, and Kasey loved it. She wished she didn't have to wear the helmet and could feel the wind sweeping through her hair, but she knew she couldn't have everything at once.

There would be time for that later.

The journey didn't take long enough for Kasey, but that was okay.

"You do realize how freaky this is. You taking me to a graveyard?" he asked.

"And it's not even Halloween."

She handed him the helmet. Her legs were a little shaky from the vibration of the bike. Holding onto Chip to keep herself steady, she opened the gates and took him down to meet her family.

"I wanted you to meet my family. I know it's pretty ... morbid, but my mother, father, and brother."

She turned to look at him, and she saw the pain on his face. "What? What is it?" she asked.

"I wish I could have met them, baby. That they could see I'm going to take care of you for the rest of my life."

"I know you are, and I'd like to believe that wherever they are, they'll know."

Chip moved up behind her, wrapping his arms around her waist. He pressed a kiss to her neck and she sighed, sinking into his touch.

"Is this where you come to?" he asked.

"Sometimes. I don't get out here as often as I'd like, but I make do with what I can." She stroked his hands, loving his touch.

"Do you talk to them?"

"Yes."

"Then introduce us. I don't think it's totally weird. Just a little."

She chuckled. "Mom, Dad, Shamus, I'd like you to meet my man, Rufus Jones, also known as Chip. We're going to be getting married soon, and I'm so happy. I'm so in love, and he makes me feel like everything was worth it." Glancing over her shoulder, she looked into his eyes. "I know without a doubt at all that you would love him, because I know that he loves me more than anything, and he'll never let anything happen to me."

He stroked her cheek. "She's the best person in the world, and even if you can't hear me, I know she is. I'm going to love and protect her for the rest of my life. I'm not going to let her go, and she will always be mine. The love of my life. The woman I want to share my entire life with."

Tears filled her eyes, as she felt his words deep in her heart.

"I love you," he said.

"I love you, too."

He pressed a kiss to her lips. "Thank you so much for bringing me here, and for also giving me the pleasure and trust of riding with me, Kasey."

She held him a little tighter, knowing there was never going to be any greater feeling in the world, not one.

Epilogue

That summer

The build-up to Chip and Kasey's wedding was a raving success for Holly and Mary's food blog. It had even taken over from the arrival of two babies. Zoe gave birth to her and Raoul's son, John, and Mary gave birth to her and Pike's second child, Thomas. On the big day itself, Chip was getting tired of all the camera shots, and he knew Kasey wouldn't be too pleased either.

Their wedding was taking place in the back yard, which had once again been transformed so there were aisles, and lots of white fabric and flowers were everywhere. It was beautiful, so he couldn't complain, especially as Holly and Mary had been the ones to take care of it.

"Are you nervous?" Pie asked, standing beside him as best man.

"No, I'm not nervous. I'm hoping she doesn't make a run for it at the last minute," Chip said.

"That's not going to happen. She loves you too much to run."

Before he could say anything else, music began to play, and it was a soft melody, not something he was used to. Lindsey and the old ladies made their way down the aisle and seeing as she didn't have anyone to give her away, Kasey had asked Crazy if he'd do the honors.

Over the years the club had become a part of her life, and he knew they were her family. Crazy handed her over, and Chip took her hand, staring into her eyes as they stepped in front of the priest.

Surrounded by his club, and his loved ones, he married Kasey to him, and to the club.

Pictures were taken as they declared themselves

husband and wife, and the club had a leather jacket which Chip gave to Kasey, declaring her his property.

He didn't let her out of his sight, keeping her by his side as they were congratulated. Mary and Holly were still in charge, so when the time came for their first dance, both women pulled them onto the dance floor.

"Shall we agree not to let them host our birthday parties?" Kasey asked, whispering.

"Agreed. I thought we were getting the better deal letting them do everything."

"And now it's like they're possessed. They keep pulling." Even as they complained, they were both smiling.

"So, Mrs. Kasey Rufus Jones, what do you plan to do for the next fifty years?" he asked.

"Let's see. I think I plan to be the perfect wife, and drive my perfect husband crazy."

"You know what, that sounds like the best thing in the world."

He kissed her lips, knowing that whatever happened, they were going to be the best fifty years of their life.

The End

www.samcrescent.com

BESTSELLING BBW ROMANCE
SPICY ROMANCE FOR REAL WOMEN

SAM CRESCENT

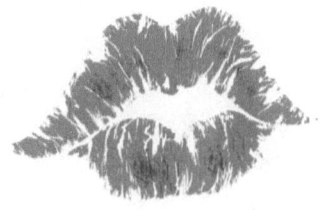

EVERNIGHT PUBLISHING ®

www.evernightpublishing.com